Murder & Mayhem

KP STAFFORD

Chapter 1

Four weeks ago, my life was planned out. Working as a legal researcher for a big name lawyer in Boston allowed me to pursue my own law degree while honing my skills. It was my father's plan. The legal field was intriguing, but I can't say it was my dream job.

My dad had taken an early vacation from his corporate job so he and my mom could spend their twenty-seventh anniversary in some remote jungle.

Having the house to myself the last few weeks of summer vacation felt liberating, although I'd started to feel a bit lonely. I questioned my career choice. Not that I had much choice since telling my father it wasn't my choice of jobs wouldn't go over very well.

The majority of the people I came in contact with were scumbags. Rich men, but still scumbags. I didn't want to deal with getting those types off of serious charges.

Fate stepped in and gave me the change I didn't expect. A phone call at two in the morning.

"Miss Danforth, this is Inspector so and so." He said his name. I didn't catch it. He continued, "I regret to inform you that the plane your parents were on has crashed in the middle of the jungle. There were no survivors."

"What?" I sat straight up in the bed. "Oh my gosh. Are you sure? They were on flight 131."

"Yes, ma'am, we're sure. The plane had started its

descent to land, there was bad weather."

After laying in bed sobbing for hours, I called my job to tell them I wouldn't be in.

"Oh, Alexis, that is so awful," the secretary said. "Let me patch you through to Dan."

Dan Matthews was a top lawyer. He could be a stern man, but not generally without compassion. He did have the personality of a lawyer though. I relayed the news, he gave his condolences and cleared his throat. An odd feeling washed over me, something was wrong. "Is there something else, Mr. Matthews?"

"Alexis, I hate to give you the news at a time like this, but I was going to tell you when you came in today."

"What is it?" I asked, not really wanting to know.

"I won't be needing a researcher anymore. You'll get a severance pay, but the position has been dropped by the firm."

I hung up the phone, rolled over in bed and bawled like a baby. In a matter of hours, my whole world had fallen apart. Being an only child with no family left, there was no one I could turn to. I was alone.

The estate manager called and insisted I get through the paperwork to tie up loose ends. I trudged up the staircase into the attic. It felt like the only place to be. My mother loved the attic and would sit up there for hours reading books, sewing or doing whatever else captured her fancy.

Looking around, I spied mom's old hat box. It had pink Victorian roses on the outside and was tied with a pink ribbon. As I approached the box, I heard mom's voice, "This is where I keep all of my magical treasures. One day, when you're older, you can have a peek inside."

I'd forgotten that memory. At twenty-five, I had long been old enough. I squatted down in front of the box which was wedged in between a few other items. It took a bit of work to wiggle it around until it dislodged from its home in the corner.

Our lives were covered with dust. Mom was always meticulous about things, even cleaning the attic. It had been awhile since she'd been up here. I looked at her treasure box. She always laughed that she kept all of her secrets in there. Secrets of fairies and magical worlds. Dad was annoyed by it, but I never knew why. My heart pinched as I untied the pink ribbon and wondered if fairies would fly out. I pulled off the lid and set it aside. Inside there were several items, but a small notebook caught my eye. I flipped through some pages with shaky hands. Sobs escaped my already tired and tormented body.

I laid on the floor of the attic, curled into a ball and cried for over an hour. After that, anger set in. Anger about the lies my parent's had told me. Now they were dead and I couldn't tell them how mad I was. My *dead* grandmother was alive and still living in our hometown, a little more than an hour away. I threw the little book back into the box, "How could my parents do this to me?" I screamed at the top of my lungs.

I went downstairs and logged into some legal and county record sites hoping to find something. I'd been told at the age of twelve that my grandmother had died. This was shortly after moving to the city. *That explains why we didn't go to the funeral.* It didn't take long for reality to set in. Over half of my life had been a lie. I reached for the phone and dialed the number listed in the yellow pages.

Two weeks after the death of my parents, I was back in my hometown. I didn't remember much about it since I was eleven when we left. Trying to figure out why my parents had uprooted us was driving me nuts. Grams was hush-hush about the whole deal. She started to tell me about a fight between her and my dad, but quickly changed the subject. I spent days with my mind spinning.

I needed to decide if I was staying, and if so, I needed to get reacquainted with the place. The fisherman's wharf was one memory I had and loved it when Grams would take me there as a child. It was mostly a bunch of shacks for the men who fished for a living, but you could also get an ice cream cone or homemade New England fudge to enjoy while you looked out across the sea. This area wasn't a tourist spot, but a few of the locals tried to make them feel welcome when they did venture to this side of the inlet. The other side of the town was a huge tourist mecca.

Grams always said the sea was a great place to cast off your concerns and worries. I figured it was a good time to do that, so I headed down the long pier to the ice cream shack, ordered a chocolate chip cone and plopped myself on the bench. Growing up in Boston I could've gone to the ocean anytime I wanted, but after hearing of Gram's *so called* death, I couldn't bring myself to go. It was our special place and it didn't seem right to go. Something changed in me that year. I stopped being a little girl and set my mind to being some kind of professional. My father stepped in and decided I'd be a lawyer.

I had stopped dreaming of magical places. Taking a deep breath in to let the salty air tingle my senses, I thought maybe it was time to start dreaming again.

Grams had left my bedroom exactly as it was when I was eleven. In a way it was sweet, but on the other hand, *I'm not that little girl any more.*

"You'll always be that little girl."

A voice from behind startled me. I whirled around to see Grams standing there. "Grams, how did you know I was here?"

Grams nonchalantly waved her hand in the air, "I saw you sitting here." She came around and sat down beside me.

I gave her a puzzled look, "Okay, so how did you just read my mind?"

Grams chuckled, "Some people just think really loud, child."

I licked the ice cream cone, unsure if I believed that. Surely Grams had some kind of special powers. She always knew things. "I don't feel like that little girl. This place used to feel magical to me. Now I'm grown and it just feels like another place on earth, nothing special, other than the memories."

"Nothing wrong with memories. The magic is still here, you'll remember it soon enough."

"Peyton says I'm too anal, but she's never been away from here. She doesn't know the real world."

"Ah, don't be so quick to decide what someone else has been through, or not. Peyton is a lot smarter than you think."

Ice cream drips ran down my fingers. I hurried to lick them off. "I'm so mad at Dad for taking us away from this place. Why did he do it? Why did they tell me you

8

were dead? Why.." My voice and thoughts trailed off.

"He was doing what he thought was right. We can't judge a person for that."

"Maybe."

"Never you mind about that. You be mad for a bit and then let it go. It won't do you no good to hang on to it." Grams rubbed the back of my head like she did when I was a little girl. It made me feel special again. "And now I have to get back to the shop before the town's people think I've gone out of business. You come by later for a visit." Grams got up and hurried off.

I turned to ask her what time to stop by, but she was nowhere in sight. The pier was too long for a person to just disappear that quickly. I began to wonder if the old woman had even been there until I saw the pink flower on the bench next to me. They were always Gram's favorite. Maybe the elderly woman was in better shape than I thought. Maybe I didn't come here to take care of her in her "old age." Maybe I was actually here to find my own self again.

I finished the ice cream and sat back to listen to the sea gulls squawking as they swooped to have dinner on a small school of fish not far from the dock. I had missed these times. Life here had been simple.

After a week visiting with Grams, I decided to drop my classes and stay in Cryptic Cove. Grams lined up a job for me as secretary to the town constable.

The most exciting thing on day one of my new job was meeting old Bessie down at the donut shop. She never meets a stranger and if she knows your family, she has tales to tell for hours. It seems my Grams was quite the character back in her youth. Apparently, the constable's office is also the town gossip line. If people weren't ringing the phone, they were coming in for a visit to tell the latest news.

My second day on the job got a little more interesting. I was staring at the cafe across the street. My attention was captured by a good-looking man opening the door. I suddenly had an urge for breakfast. He was about six feet two, dark hair and a gorgeous smile. He held the door for others entering the establishment. *Oh, he's such a gentleman.* You don't see that much these days. A man with those looks could be dangerous for a gal's heart. I suppose if I can watch this guy every day, my job won't be so bad.

The phone rang, jolting me out of my daydream with Mr. Hottie. I composed myself before picking up the receiver, "Constable's Office. How can I help you?"

"Hello? Is this John's place?" The voice inquired. She sounded as old as the hills.

"Yes, ma'am, this is."

"Oh good. I thought I'd rang the wrong number. Not used to anyone else answering. Are you new?"

"Yes, this is my second day."

"Well, who are you, girl?"

I'd been in town long enough to know that giving my own name meant nothing to these people, "I'm Velda's granddaughter."

"Oh, you're little Lexi." She screeched in delight, "So glad to have you back. It's been such a long time, hasn't it?"

"Yes, ma'am." I caught myself rolling my eyes. Even if

the lady couldn't see me, it was rude. At least it wasn't a personal meeting or I'd be embraced in a bear hug. These people liked to hug. It was sweet, but it could be annoying.

"I remember your little pigtails and you had the cutest freckles across your nose."

I sat back in my chair. I'd learned on my first day that you couldn't rush these calls. They'd eventually remember why they called, or maybe not. A few of them thought I had called them. I had to giggle to myself. It really was a charming place.

"Anyway dear," she said, breaking my thought, "I'll be bringing the eggs into town later today and I'll need John to help me unload them." She took in a breath, her excitement seemed to take the wind out of her, but she continued without missing too much of a beat, "Burt will load them here, but you know him, he only comes to town for special occasions and church on Sunday."

"Yes ma'am," I said reaching for a pen and paper, "I'm leaving him a note now."

"Okay then, you have a good day dear. I have to get back to the morning chores." She hung up.

I put the phone down just as John came through the front door, "And how are you this morning, young lady?" He asked with a smile that beamed across the whole room.

"Great!" I replied. "I have a message for you."

"Ooh, some crime I need to go solve?" He had a glimmer of hope in his eyes.

No, just a lady reminding you about the eggs today."

"Oh good. That will be Mrs. June. She brings eggs in every week for the local market. She doesn't want anything for them." He pondered for a moment, "She must have several hundred chickens on that farm. I've never seen so many chickens in my life." He chuckled, "Folks 'round here call her the chicken lady.

I nodded my head.

John sat donuts down in front of me. This town would be the death of me. One can only consume so many donuts. I looked at John and noted he was still thin. He must workout. I'd have to start running again to keep the pounds off. I hadn't found one whole grain muffin in the whole town.

John took his note and headed to his inner office. John Ballard was the town constable, although best I could tell, he mostly rescued cats out of trees, hauled eggs and occasionally stopped a feud between the town's people.

I sat back in the chair and flipped through a catalog, hoping some excitement would jump out at me. It didn't. I glanced across the street to see if Mr. Hottie was still having breakfast. He was laughing with the waitress. *He's probably a big flirt.* That's been my experience with guys that good-looking.

After one week, I realized there are some strange people in this town, but it kept me from moping around over the loss of my parents. I guess I'd have to get used to life in a small town where the biggest news is whose chickens escaped or who won Bingo last week.

Chapter 2

Monday of the second week started off pretty normal. The town was bustling with people getting back to work after a relaxing weekend. By ten in the morning, I'd gotten about six phone calls from local business owners. Yes, the gossip box had to catch up on the weekend news, or at least, inform me of it. This job may turn out to be quite amusing if it doesn't drive me crazy first. I now see why John wanted help. He couldn't get any work done holding a phone to his ear half the day.

I'd just settled in for the mid-morning donut consumption when Grams burst through the door, out of breath and frazzled. She was a mess. I got up and walked around the desk to help seat her in the over-stuffed chair by the window. "What's wrong Grams? You look like you've seen a ghost."

"Earnest and Wilma Swanson," she gasped out between breaths, "are missing!"

"What?" I perked up some. It wasn't nice to think someone was missing, but it was exciting at this point of my new life. "How do you know this?"

"I can't find them anywhere! They're just gone."

John came out of his office, hearing the disturbance. Maybe he finally had a mystery to check out. He walked over to put his hand on Grams' shoulder. Calm visibly washed over her. "Oh John, they're gone. I just know it."

"Who's gone?"

"The Swanson's. I can't find them anywhere."

"Now Velda, you know how they can be. They probably took the Saturday bus into the city and haven't returned yet." He looked at me for assurance.

"Yes, Grams. I'm sure they've just gone to the city." I bit my bottom lip.

Grams crinkled her nose and looked at John, "You know better than that. They were meeting me this morning and they never miss a meeting. Besides, the whole town would be talking about their trip if that had happened."

I looked at John again. The look on his face told me the gossip box would have reported something as monumental as this.

"Don't worry, Velda," John said as he rubbed Grams' shoulder, "When did you see them last?"

"The bridge game on Friday night. We played a little late. They were going to walk home like they normally do. It was so late, I insisted they let me drive them."

"Did you see them go into their home?"

Grams looked confused. "I can't remember. I know they walked towards the door, so I just backed out of the driveway and left."

"Lexi and I will get on the horn and find out what happened." He looked at me, "Can you call the bus station and ask if they took a bus over the weekend. I'll get your grandmother home and then figure out a plan when I get back."

"Sure. Anything you need."

I had gotten to know John pretty well the past week. He was a jovial man, but he wasn't amused at what this could mean if the couple was missing. It would be the biggest news this town had seen since...I tried to think back to something from my childhood. I tried not to gasp when I remembered that my Aunt Agatha had disappeared nearly thirty years ago. That would definitely put the town on edge. Many of these people lived here back then too.

Grams argued she wasn't going home. Instead, she headed to her shop, Crystal Scents. Grams' candles were unique. In the bottom of each jar candle was a crystal or gemstone. John escorted her out the door, trying to get her to take the day off.

I called the old guy at the bus station. He assured me the Swanson's hadn't taken a trip in two months. I didn't know who else to call waiting for John to return so I called my best friend from childhood, Peyton Lewis, to tell her the news. Our friendship picked back up immediately on my return. I expected it to feel strained, but it was almost magical the way we instantly took to each other during our reunion. I didn't like that the gossip box had rubbed off on me so quickly, but it was nice to have a friend to talk to these days.

After I hung up from talking to Peyton, the phone rang four times, all people who had heard about the disappearance. There's no need for the newspaper in this town, although old man Jordan prints one daily. He was the second person to call to ask if I had any information he could quote in the next edition. The town's people definitely had more information than John and me at this point. One person asked if we'd checked the shoals, they might have walked off the cliff. One suggested the aliens had returned and snatched them up from their beds. *Returned? Was there a first time?*

John walked through the door about thirty minutes later. A furrowed brow replaced his usual expression. He sat down in the chair across from my desk and rubbed his chin, "I don't suppose you found out anything or know what to do next?" His tone was distant.

I shook my head no. I had no idea where to start with an investigation. Apparently John wasn't too qualified himself. Lost cats were more up to his speed these days. I'd have to be a quick study. I guess research and being nosey through the daily gossip might pay off.

John smiled, "As stubborn as a mule that woman is."

I felt my brow crease, unsure of what he meant by the remark.

"Your grandmother. She's always said she can't have the whole town going off balance if she's not at work."

Grams could be hard to figure out. The town wouldn't fall apart if she took the day off. *Would it?*

I looked over at John and feared he would rub a hole in his chin. "What are you thinking?"

He let out a long sigh, "This is going to bring up a lot of old memories for the town's people."

"You mean Aunt Agatha?"

"You remember that?"

"I didn't at first, but I'm starting to."

John stood up. "I was volunteer Search and Rescue in those days. We combed the woods for days, hoping to find her."

"Who led the investigation back then?"

"Some old chap. He's long been dead now." He gave me a puzzled look. "You don't think the two are related," he trailed off, "after all these years?"

"Probably not. Just thought if you could look at that old case file, it might give you some direction now."

"It could. The county handled most of that. I'll go on over to Washburn and see what I can find out. In the meantime, would you like to run some errands for me?"

"Okay. What can I do?"

"Can you head up to Hayden's Ridge? It would be courteous to let Bernie Copeland know two of his tenants are missing."

"Sure."

John left the office and I locked the door before I headed to the retirement village.

Chapter 3

I hadn't intended for John to send me to Hayden's Ridge Retirement Village, but he said the owner could be a "spiteful old codger" when things weren't going his way. John thought it'd be best to send a *cute young lady*, as he called me. It couldn't hurt to use some of my charm on an old guy. I decided to play it safe and be a concerned citizen delivering the news. I'd also wing it and ask some basic questions to begin with.

The drive up to the village was pleasant. It felt like early fall in the air. I thought about my first round of questions and realized I was getting more apprehensive about the whole thing. *Just stay calm and relax Alexis*, I told myself. I had to laugh at not being called by my formal name in the last month. Everyone here knew me as Lexi. No matter how many times I tried to correct them to use my real name, they ignored me and continued to call me by my childhood nickname. I guess I should just give up. I also thought it best to introduce myself as Lexi. This wasn't a formal questioning, so no point in making it seem like it was. I was starting to like Lexi anyway. As Alexis, my life and career were planned out in the legal field. As Lexi, it was like learning to walk on new legs without any direction as to where I was headed. Most people might find this feeling to be liberating. To me, it was scary. It felt like I was a side show in some carnival.

It was only a short drive up the hillside. Many folks walked this road to get exercise. Maybe I should have walked and burned off some of those donuts. I spotted the gate with brick and a wrought iron fence ahead.

Through the gate was a beautiful little village. This was a quaint looking neighborhood with bungalows and cottages. It set on top of a cliff, hence the name Hayden's Ridge. I assumed it overlooked the ocean, but I couldn't tell from the street view. The office looked like a mansion at the end of a circle drive. The homes lined the main street leading up to the office. The sign on the front indicated it was also the community center, game room, recreation area and apartments for the elderly. I secretly wondered what it cost the elderly to live here. It was definitely a place for people who had money. I made a note of that to myself to mention to John. Sometimes a money trail is the easiest to follow in criminal cases. Not that this was a criminal case, or that I had any experience in these matters, but I had a bad feeling in my gut. I'd only been here a few weeks, but you get a feel for a place like this pretty quickly and I didn't feel too good about finding this elderly couple.

I waited in the sitting area for over half an hour. His secretary kept assuring me it would only be a few minutes. The feeling in my gut wasn't as irritating as her staring at me between fielding phone calls. The way she looked at me made me wonder if she knew something or wanted to tell me something. I was getting ready to question her when Mr. Copeland opened his office door and asked me to step inside.

He seated me in the over-stuffed chair in front of his desk, as I told him who I was.

"What can I do for such a lovely young woman?" he asked as he went around the desk and sat in the leather office chair. "Are you looking for a place for a loved one? We have some beautiful homes here in the village."

"Mr. Copeland-," I began.

"Call me Bernie," he interrupted.

"Bernie," I said even though it didn't feel right, "I'm here to ask some questions about the Swanson's."

"The Swanson's?" He seemed puzzled like he was searching his mind to remember who they were. "Oh, yes, Earnest, and his wife, Velma."

"Wilma," I corrected.

"Yes, yes. What kind of information are you looking for? You know, I'm under strict confidentiality laws." Throwing that last bit in piqued my interest, did he have something to hide?

"Yes sir, but they seem to be missing."

"Is that so? They've probably gone off on holiday or something. Our retiree's like to travel a lot."

"Yes, we thought of that, but there's no record of them leaving town. We wondered if they had told you or one of their neighbors about a trip? Can you think of any reason they'd just disappear?"

The look on his face hardened. So much for thinking nice legs would make an impression. One mention of a possible disappearance and his whole demeanor changed.

"Our tenants are not prisoners here. They're allowed to come and go as they please. It's not my business to keep up with all of them."

John had suspected the man wouldn't be happy about losing two of his residents. John was wrong. The man wasn't too concerned about it. When I asked if we could have access to their residence, he only had two words for me. Court order.

I wasn't liking Mr. Copeland. I guess he couldn't keep up with everyone at the village, but he could pay a little more attention to his residents.

Once I got in my car I pulled out a notepad and started writing. I still had more questions than answers. I grabbed my keys off the passenger seat to put them in the ignition. The door to the retirement center opened and Bernie Copeland headed to his car. He was visibly irritated and in a hurry. *Should I follow him?*

Chapter 4

This quiet little town had been disrupted overnight. I was in need of a quiet evening so my best friend, Peyton Lewis came by with her daughter, Paisley. We enjoyed wine and pizza while sitting on the back deck watching Paisley feed carrots to some rabbits. It was cute the way they came up to her. She was nine years old and exceptionally bright. Even though Peyton had begun motherhood at the age of sixteen, she had done a fantastic job of raising her little girl.

As I watched the rabbits come up to her, I was reminded how strange this place could be. It was charming and had lovely people, but it also had a mysterious undertone to it. Even more mysterious was an old couple disappearing.

The gossip train started as soon as I got into the office the next morning. I had needed the relaxing evening, but I was starting to feel like I needed a whole weekend. I was starting to question if I'd made the right decision about quitting school and moving back here. I wasn't cut out to solve crimes, legal paperwork was more my style, even though I didn't want to admit it.

One of the daily callers had already heard that I was *helping* John on the case and asked if we'd followed the insurance trail. They'd seen it the night before on a popular television show and thought it might be a good lead. They were also sure to mention that the new insurance guy, Jake Donovan was the nephew to Bernie Copeland. He'd only been in town a few months.

I thought about that after I hung up the phone. I was already wanting to get away from the phone and thought a trip to the insurance agency was in order. I let John know what I was doing and headed out the door.

I had barely gotten seated in the waiting area when the receptionist told me I could go on in to see Mr. Donovan. I thanked her and headed into his office. I expected to find an older gentleman, as Mr. Copeland seemed to be close to retirement age. What I didn't expect was to come face to face with Mr. Hottie from the diner. I felt sure I'd just had one of those hot flashes. At least now he had a name and he wasn't a tourist. I could inform Peyton of that bit. My heart was racing as I stood just inside the door, staring at the man. My mouth gaped open as he looked up from his desk and smiled at me. My knees went weak. I hadn't felt a teenage-like crush in about ten years. I suddenly remembered what it was like. *Regain your composure and be professional. Breathe, don't forget to breathe, Lexi.* I felt my face go flush as I stepped forward to introduce myself.

"Miss Danforth, it's nice to finally meet you." He extended his hand towards me, "It is Miss, correct?"

"Uh-huh," was all I could manage to get out. Yeah, real professional. I took in a deep breath as I reached to shake his hand. Tingles coursed through my body when my hand made contact with his. "I'm sorry, yes, it's Miss."

He motioned for me to sit in the chair, "Jake. Call me Jake. I don't stand on formalities here."

I eased myself down into the chair, afraid my legs would give out at any moment.

"What can I do for you, Miss Danforth? Are you here to start an insurance policy?"

"Uhm, no, actually." I had a line of questions in my head before I got here. Now, my mind was a complete blank. I didn't know where to even start. "I'm helping Constable Ballard."

"Yes, I've heard about that."

"News travels fast around here. I work for him. He's got a lot of stuff to take care of and asked if I'd help him ask a few questions."

"I've seen you in his office from the diner across the street."

He's seen me? Had he been spying on me, like I'd been spying on him? I was feeling like a teenage girl. *Get a grip Lexi. Get focused, get this business over with and get out of his office as soon as possible.* "Well, as you've probably heard, an elderly couple is missing. I was wondering if they had some kind of life insurance policy."

"Yes, they do."

I waited for him to say more. He didn't. "Is it a large amount? Is there a beneficiary?"

"Yes."

Again, I waited. It was obvious he wasn't going to give me any more than I actually asked for. "Can you tell me who that is?"

"No." He paused and stood up," I have confidentiality laws to follow. Unless you have a court order, I can't release any information." He walked around and sat on the edge of his desk.

"Would you like to have dinner with me?"

His question threw me for a loop. How could he think about a dinner date at a time like this? My nerves were already jangled. A whole evening with him would ruin my resolve for sure. "Mr. Donovan, I don't think this is the time for planning a date."

He stood up. His tall frame hovered over me. Like I needed to feel any smaller at this moment. I sat there staring up at him. Should I stand up too? Was he ready to usher me out of his office?

"Let me show you out, Miss Danforth."

I had my answer. So much for getting any information from him.

"Someone reported seeing them in your office a week ago. Can you tell me about that?"

"They were just updating some things." He headed towards the door.

I stood up and noticed the file on his desk. It belonged to the Swanson's. I turned to look at him. "You don't find it odd that they've disappeared?"

He stopped and looked at me. "Yes, I do. I think it's horrible. I'm just an insurance guy. It's not my place to keep up with every client I have."

"You're rather callous about it."

"I have work to do. Bring me a court order and I'll gladly share what I can about their file."

"A court order could take days since no immediate family has reported them missing." I walked towards the door.

"If it makes you feel better, their insurance doesn't pay unless they're deceased."

I glared at him, "No, it doesn't make me feel any better."

"Are you sure you won't have dinner with me?" His smile was infectious. A girl could get lost in that smile. No wonder the waitress always looked like she was in a good mood when he came to the diner. I headed out the door quickly, ready to get away from him before I turned into a drooling schoolgirl, "Thanks for your time." I said over my shoulder as I hurried past the receptionist's desk.

Chapter 5

I went home that night completely annoyed. The quiet evening I'd enjoyed the night before seemed like a dream at this point. As I pulled into the drive, I saw lights on in the house. Grams must be home. She was certainly active for her age and rarely came home before dark. The sun was just setting behind her two-story Victorian home. Dragging myself up the steps and onto the porch, I opened the front door and was hit by wonderful aromas. Ah, the smell of Grams cooking. It took me back to being eleven years old when she would cook all of my favorites.

I kicked off my shoes and let my nose lead me to the kitchen. Grams was chattering to herself. She seemed restless. Considering two of her best friends were missing, it was understandable. "It smells good in here, Grams."

She turned with a startled look on her face, "Oh dear," she said as she placed her hand on her chest, "I didn't hear you come in."

"Maybe that's because you were talking to yourself."

She waved her hand towards the back door, "I was talking to Baxter."

Looking up, I saw him on his perch next to his pet door that had been built in over the back door. "Hey, Baxter. How's the crow's life this evening." He cawed out. My guess was it meant things were good. I turned to Grams, "I'm sorry Grams. I should have looked around before thinking you were talking to yourself."

Gram's laughed. "Well, I have been known to talk to

myself, but I'm not going senile yet."

I went to the cupboard to get the dishes for setting the table. Grams stopped me before I could pull the plates out. "No dear, use the good stuff tonight." She pointed to her china cabinet. This set had been in the family probably since the first set of china had been sold. It was rare and expensive. I was always afraid to touch it.

"Are you sure Grams?"

She looked at me with a hint of sadness in her eyes. "Yes. Life is too short to not use the best dishes more often."

I set the table and poured us both a glass of white wine even though I wasn't sure what we were eating. According to Grams, when it came to white wine, you could have it with anything. She placed the food on the table and we both sat down. She'd made a roast, meatloaf, gravy, mashed potatoes and her famous homemade biscuits. I could already tell I'd overstuff myself.

We ate in silence for a bit. I finally reached over and touched Grams' arm. "How are you holding up, Grams?"

She put her fork down. "I'm doing okay, sweetie. It's just been a long time since...since anything like this has happened here."

"Is it bringing back memories of Aunt Agatha?"

A tear formed in her eye. "Yes. I know it's been twenty-five years, but I still miss her so." She wiped her eyes. "A lot of my friends are reliving the same old memories too. It's hard on all of us."

Baxter swooped down and landed on the table. I could have sworn he was trying to console Grams. She looked at him and smiled. "I'm okay Baxter." She pinched off a piece of biscuit. "Have a little treat."

He took the piece of bread and flew back to his perch.

Grams looked back at me, "Do you and John have any leads yet?"

"Not really. Everything so far is a dead end. Mr. Copeland could care less that his residents are missing. He told me to get a court order if we wanted to look at their home.." I trailed off for a moment. "I guess I'll go see the Magistrate tomorrow and find out about that. She's the closest thing to a judge here."

"She can be something to deal with. She's a good woman, just very serious when it comes to her job. Don't let her get under your skin."

"Thanks for the tip." I refilled my wine glass and sat back in the chair. "I went to see Jake Donovan too."

"What does he have to do with it?"

"John wanted to find out about an insurance policy. He was about as helpful as Copeland and told me to get a court order."

He's such a nice young man," Grams said. I could have sworn she swooned. "He would make a nice young fella for you, dear."

I rolled my eyes. Not that he wasn't attractive, but I didn't need Grams playing match-maker. "He did ask me out."

"So when is the big date?" Grams got a sparkle in her eye.

"I didn't agree to go."

"Why not?"

"I don't know. He kinda made me mad about the court order. I should have accepted, though. He might have given me some kind of information about their insurance. I think I blew it, but he did have their policy on his desk."

"I'm sure he'll ask again. Don't fret none. You can ask Mavis about that court order too when you see her tomorrow.

I laughed. "She'll probably find it odd that I need so many."

"Oh, I'm sure she knows the drill. I can't imagine she doesn't have some kind of knowledge of the law, considering what her job is."

"True."

Grams and I got the kitchen cleaned up and took our final glass of wine out to the back porch. We saw a few rabbits. They were probably looking for Paisley and her carrots.

It was nice to enjoy this time with Grams, just the two of us. I could feel a definite sadness about her these days, but she stayed busy. She stayed busy all the time, but even more so lately. I don't think I've ever known a woman as spry as she is at her age. The years have been kind to her. That's for sure.

I looked over and noticed she was staring at the full moon and whispering. I vaguely remember her doing that when I was a little girl. I don't remember if she ever told me why she does it. I didn't feel tonight was a good time to ask. So I sat there, staring at the moon with her.

Chapter 6

The alarm sounded at 6:00 am. It was just getting light outside after breakfast so I decided to take a walk through the woods. I needed to get my thoughts together before tackling my day and the barrage of phone calls that would await me at the office.

Peyton and I loved these woods as kids. There were still many of the old trails left. The main ones led to different places, so you really couldn't get lost. At least, I didn't think so in my younger days.

Baxter tagged along with me. He could be such a strange bird, but I didn't mind his company. At times, I preferred to be with him instead of people. He never asked a slew of questions. He just listened to me talk things out with myself, much like I'd heard Grams doing last night. From time to time he'd reply. *Like he was really listening.*

We meandered through the woods for forty-five minutes or more, not paying attention to where I was going. I looked around to see if anything seemed familiar or if I heard traffic from any of the streets. I'd never been this far into the woods since I'd returned. Baxter flew by, nearly grazing my shoulder. He landed on an outcropping of rocks off to the right. There was a small area where you could get under the ledge of the rocks. He squawked and glided down to the ground. He was pulling at something in the leaves that had piled up under the rocks. It was probably a worm, judging by the looks of it. Baxter's noise-making got louder and he was really after something. I walked down the embankment to inspect his treasure.

A gold chain caught my eye. The soil was loose so I brushed some of it away, jumping back when I realized it was a bracelet. And it was attached to a woman's hand. *Oh my gosh, please don't let this be Mrs. Swanson.* I dug for my cell phone to see if I had a signal. There was none.

I walked for half an hour before I got a signal, almost to Grams' house. I dialed John's office. Relief eased over me some when he answered on the second ring. "John, this is Lexi. You need to come to the woods behind the house. I've found..." I trailed off. All I'd seen was a hand. I couldn't be sure it was a whole body.

"Lexi, speak up. What have you found?"

"I think it's a dead body. I saw a hand in the dirt."

"Oh, my. I'll be there as soon as I can. Meet me at the house."

By the time I finished walking the short distance to the house to meet John, Baxter flew in behind me, scaring the crap out of me. My nerves were on edge.

Within twenty minutes John pulled in with a county cop. Grams came out of the house as he stepped out of the car. He looked at her and shook his head. "Velda, what are you doing here?"

"I live here! What are you doing here?"

"Lexi has found something. I need you to stay here until we can check it out."

"Is it the Swanson's?" She asked and then looked at me. "Lexi, is it them?"

"I don't know Grams. Do what John says and just

stay here. It's a good ways into the woods."

John turned to face Grams again, "Please Velda. We don't need you traipsing off through the woods. It could be a long walk. Stay here."

"John Ballard, I've walked these woods my entire life. I am not some worn-out, old piece of shoe leather." And with that, she walked right past him and headed off into the woods.

I caught up with her while John and the other cop pulled shovels out of their car trunks. I knew it was useless to try and talk sense into my grandmother, so I just paced in, along beside her, figuring the men would catch up soon enough.

Grams shot a look of aggravation at me, "Don't say a word, child."

"I'm not saying anything, Grams."

"I'm not sitting around the house waiting."

"I noticed," I said. I wanted to chuckle at her determination, but under the circumstances, it wasn't appropriate.

John and the deputy caught up. John looked over at me, "How far into the woods did you go?"

"I'm not real sure. It was almost a straight line, though. It was actually Baxter who discovered it, so it's a bit off the trail."

We walked on for a bit. When I noticed the trail was starting to follow a ridge, I told John we were close. The hand I'd found was under a rock formation. It should be easy to spot, but I noticed this area had several formations on the hillside.

Baxter landed in a tree just up ahead. Grams looked at him, "Baxter, take us to the trinket you found earlier."

I gave Grams a quizzical look but she ignored it. I know she's not senile, but expecting a crow to understand what she says is just a bit odd.

Baxter flew up the trail and started squawking. Grams picked up the pace and the rest of us fell in behind her. John picked up his pace, intent on keeping her from finding the hand first.

We stopped and looked down the ridge where Baxter was. John and the deputy made their way down to Baxter. Grams tried to follow, but I grabbed her arm, "Grams, let's let John do his job. Okay?"

She shot me a look of annoyance but stayed put. I looked at the bird and wondered if he did understand everything we said. I stifled a chuckle at how silly I was starting to think since being back.

John and the deputy looked around the spot where the hand was sticking out and started digging.

Chapter 7

An hour later a shallow grave was uncovered with the bodies of the Swanson's beneath the fresh earth and leaves. The coroner had arrived and was inspecting the scene. Orvel Haynes was an odd man. He reminded me of a mad scientist from old black and white films. His hair was disheveled. Grams said it had been that way as long as she could remember.

There was something strange between him and Grams when they spoke. I got the feeling she didn't like or trust him, but for some reason she tolerated him. As far as I knew, Grams had never dated anyone after the death of grandpa, but there was definitely a tension between this man and my grandmother. A tension I'd never seen her show with anyone.

The assistant ME arrived about fifteen minutes later on a four-wheeler towing a cart behind it. They had borrowed them for easy transport of the bodies out of the woods.

A few hours later I had Grams at home with a cup of hot tea. She was holding herself together pretty well. I expected her to show more despair knowing they were dead than when she announced they were missing. She was like a rock. I guessed she'd break down in her own time.

We sat in the backyard, silent for awhile. I finally broke the silence, "What's up with that creepy mortician?"

Grams looked over with an odd look on her face, "What do you mean?"

I ran my foot across the blades of grass. I wasn't real sure how to ask so I just came out with it. "There seems to be something hinky between the two of you."

Grams let out a sigh. "He was in love with Agatha. I know it seems crazy, but it's like I have a connection with her through him."

"Was she in love with him?"

"No. They dated some, but she wasn't looking for anything serious between them." She paused. "After her disappearance, he came by several times, trying to keep my spirits up, I guess." She creased her eyebrows, "I never really knew why he felt the need to do that. I was sure he loved her, though, so in a way, it did ease my mind that we were both missing her terribly." Grams reached over and patted my hand. "That's old news. Now we have this murder mess going on."

"Can you think of anyone who wanted them dead?"

"Oh heavens no. They could be feisty, but they were such a sweet couple. Always helping others out, volunteering at every event in town. I just can't imagine."

"Did they have any family who might want their money?"

"Not that I know of. They never had kids." Grams sat up in her chair and looked over at me, "Do you think this is about money?"

"I don't know, but it's one of the main reasons people kill other people."

"You should go see that Jake fella again. Try to get some answers from him."

"Grams I can't do that. It's in the hands of the county police now."

"Nonsense. He's more likely to talk to you. You should accept his dinner invitation."

Here we go again. Grams didn't know I had suspicions of Jake Donovan. Dinner with him could be enlightening or a complete disaster if he found out I wanted to investigate why he still had their insurances papers out on his desk the other day. But the fact remained this wasn't my job. I didn't need to be snooping around in people's business.

Grams looked over at me. "I guess it'll be easier getting those court orders now." She trailed off, not wanting to use the word *dead* in reference to her friends.

Chapter 8

The phone rang more than usual at the office. The whole town was in a frenzy about the death of Earnest and Wilma. John came through the door around ten and said he'd given up on trying to reach me by phone. He didn't quite grasp the concept that I have a cell number and he could reach me as long as I had a signal. He waved it off as nonsense and asked if I'd mind taking care of a few things.

By lunch time the phones had quieted down so I headed to the sandwich shop. Peyton said she'd meet me there. We liked the quietness of the sandwich shop. John had asked me to go see about the court orders after lunch.

Peyton was running late, so I ordered her the usual Club sandwich. It arrived at the table about the time she did. She started in telling me how the news had traveled and a few people had canceled their reservations for the weekend. Even more had called wanting to know if she had rooms available. People wanted to come and witness a real live murder case. Her B&B was booked solid for the next week so she was having to send people to another one in town. She was a non-stop chatter box.

"Isn't this crazy?" She finally asked. "This town has been boring my whole life and as soon as you come back, it gets very interesting." She winked.

"What are you saying? You think I'm jinxed or something?"

"Heck no. It's just like old times when we were kids

and solving all the missing stuff in school. It's sad, you know, but it's kinda cool too."

You had to love Peyton. She was a bit naive and hadn't ever ventured out of this town, but she had a bright way to looking at things, even the bad things.

"You're going to be great at figuring this out."

"Peyton, this is police business. I'm only helping John with the phones and paperwork."

"Pffft. When we were kids, you could figure anything out and you have to admit, it might be fun seeing if we figure it out before the cops do."

"I suppose you have a point."

"Good, I'll come by this evening and we can put some notes together." She stood up to gather her things before heading back to the B&B. "You want me to grab pizza?"

"No, Grams has plenty of leftovers. She went on a cooking spree the other day."

"Meatloaf?" She perked up.

"Uh-huh."

"Oh my gosh, your Grams' meatloaf is divine."

I grabbed my things and gave Peyton a hug, "It is."

The walk to the constable's office wasn't far, but I had to stop at the town magistrate's office.

Grams was right about Mavis Clark. She was not a trusting soul, questioned everything. What should have taken a few minutes to put in a request for some court orders from the judge, took nearly forty-five minutes. She had to call John to make sure the request was proper. Getting him on the phone took almost half an hour. They discussed implications of the case, although she was trying to make sure I didn't hear what she was saying. She also had issues with the county boys who'd already been in her office that morning with the same request.

She hung up the phone and looked at me with her beady eyes. They weren't really beady, I just expected them to be after all the hoops she'd put me through. "The judge has already signed off on court orders for the county cops. I can't ask him to sign off on the same papers twice."

"Then why did you call John and have me wait?"

"Just a formality." She had a despicable grin on her face. She knew she could get away with this kind of hee-hawing around and was taking great pleasure in it.

"I think you did this on purpose."

"Prove it. I'm just doing my job. If you don't like the procedures around here, then find another line of work so you don't have to deal with it."

I stood up straight and went on the defensive. "Do you know who I am?" Grams seemed to have some pull in this town and I was hoping it'd help me out.

"Yes, and that doesn't mean a hill of beans in this office, young lady." She grabbed a few papers from the counter. "Now, if you don't mind, I have a job to do." She turned and went back to her desk.

I felt deflated. It was silly to try and use my grandmother as a way to get a favor, but I'd done it and failed miserably. On the way back to John's office, I kept wondering what she had against Grams. She was the first person I'd encountered that didn't sing the praises of Velda Wheeler.

As soon as I walked into the constable's office, the phone was ringing. I dropped my things in the chair by the door and ran to pick it up. It was Grams scolding me for bringing up her name at the magistrate's office. This definitely peaked my curiosity into their past.

Chapter 9

John returned to the office soon after I did. He had a thin folder tucked under his arm and dropped it on my desk. "This is all the county boys have on Agatha's disappearance."

"I picked it up and thumbed through it. "It's not very much is it?"

"Not at all. I was sure there'd be something in there to help us work on this case."

"According to the magistrate, we're not even supposed to be working this case."

"Did she say that?"

"Well, no, but she gave me the runaround and wasn't very helpful. Said the county already had the court orders and we couldn't do anything about it."

John sat in the chair by the window, his usual upbeat personality hadn't been present in two days. "This is starting to feel just like that old case there." He said as he pointed to the file folder on my desk.

"What do you mean?"

He rubbed his chin, "We felt railroaded by the county back then. And I'm feeling railroaded now about this case."

"You think there's a connection?"

"Not really. It just seems like things haven't changed much over the past twenty-five years where county laws are concerned."

John stood up and walked to the door, "I'm going to see Bernie Copeland. This is still my town."

"That's the spirit," I said as he walked out the door.

I flipped through the file on my desk hoping to find an answer. Like John, I didn't think a twenty-five-year-old case had anything to do with this one, but this was my aunt's disappearance and I wanted to know some of the details. It took about ten minutes to skim through it. It was almost like they didn't try to find her. None of the old leads checked out. Much like the leads we had about this new case. Thinking back to the law firm I had worked at for two years, I was starting to see why lawyers were such a grumpy bunch. It was just as frustrating on the investigative end too.

The door opened bringing me out of my thoughts. Jake Donovan stood there with a concerned look on his face.

"Can I help you?"

"I came by to apologize for my behavior the other day. I'm sorry the Swanson's were found dead."

"Well, I guess you'll have to pay out on that life insurance policy now."

"Look, I was being insensitive the other day. I thought they'd just gone on a short vacation." He had a panged look on his face, "I didn't expect them to show up...dead."

"No one did, but they are."

"Let me make it up to you over dinner."

My first thought was to decline. Not only did he irritate me, but he was so good looking while being irritating, I knew too much time with him could lead to trouble. Big trouble. It could be a good chance to get him to talk. At least that's what I was hoping for. "I have plans tonight."

"How about Friday night then?"

I didn't want to seem too ambitious about it. "Let me check my calendar," I said as I pulled out my cell phone and thumbed around on it. I knew I didn't have any plans, but he didn't. "Okay, Friday sounds good."

He smiled and my heart gave a quick skip. It's a good thing I was sitting down or I'd be weak in the knees. "I'll pick you up at seven."

He turned to leave.

"Wait a minute," I called after him, "Is it casual?"

There was that smile again, but this time with a hint of mischief. "Semi-casual, maybe a bit dressy." He winked as he turned to walk out the door.

After he left I sat there worried about Friday getting here too soon. What is semi-casual? Jeans and pizza were obviously not the style or the menu. I'd have to dig through my closet to find something that doubled as casual and dressy. Maybe this wasn't such a good idea.

Chapter 10

Peyton arrived around six that evening. Paisley headed off to the living room to watch an old cartoon movie collection while we headed to the kitchen to start warming up Grams' divine meatloaf.

It had been a long day for both of us. The B&B business was hopping over the news of a murder in town. Our first order of business after popping the meatloaf and some mashed potatoes into the warming oven was to enjoy a cup of hot tea.

Peyton took a sip of tea before looking at me and digging in. "What's happened today? Do you know anything new?"

I thought for a moment, not sure where to begin. "Not really, mostly a bunch of old news."

"What do you mean? Like what?"

"John got the case file from my aunt's disappearance, but there's nothing in it."

Peyton crinkled her nose. She was really cute when she did it, but it always indicated her brain was working on something. "What do you mean? Is it related to this case?"

"No, John thought he could fish out some information or tactics as a way to look at this case. But, apparently they didn't put much thought into her disappearance back then." I stood up to start getting the food out of the oven.

Peyton grabbed some plates out of the cupboard.

"That's weird. Looks like that would have been a huge priority back then."

"I know. That's why it's so weird. The file is more like a teenage prank investigation."

We fixed our plates and sat down. I dug the file out of my bag and handed it to Peyton. "See, there's barely anything in there."

Peyton thumbed through it between bites of food. "I see they questioned people who still live here. I see Mavis Clark, that creepy mortician. But you're right. Nothing panned out and it's like they gave up." She sat the folder on the edge of the table. "What about those search warrants you were getting today?"

"Pfft!" I huffed out, blowing my bangs out of my eyes. "That went nowhere. The county guys already had them so there's nothing John and I can do."

"So, today was a total loss, huh?"

"Well, not completely. Jake came by to apologize and asked me out again."

Her eyes perked up as a coy smile crossed her face. "Annnd.."

I hesitated before answering. "We're going out Friday night."

"You don't seem too enthused."

"I do want to see if he'll tell me anything, but I'm really nervous. He said it was semi-casual and I don't have a clue what that means in this town."

"Ah. We'll go through your clothes after we eat and if we can't find anything, I'm sure I have something."

I had to laugh, Peyton has more clothes than anyone I've ever met. "I'm sure you do." I took a sip of tea. "I'm just nervous about the whole thing. He was defensive the other day like he's hiding something. I mean, why was their policy still on his desk almost a week after they'd been in to see him?"

"I don't know. Maybe it takes a few days to get stuff in order?"

"Could be, but I still think he's hiding something. I don't want him to catch on to my suspicions." I thought for a few minutes. "Maybe he's already on to me. Why else would he come by the office acting so nice and asking me out again?"

"You'll be fine," Peyton replied.

"Well, there's more."

"You look worried. What is it?"

"John went to see that Bernie Copeland today. He got kind of irate with John."

"What does that mean?"

They've both gotten testy when questioned. What if they're in some insurance scam together?"

"All the more reason for you to go on that date. Let's go find you something to wear."

As Peyton and I were going through my closet we heard the door slam downstairs and the voices of Grams and John. We went to see what was happening. Grams was pacing the living room and was madder than I'd ever seen her. She looked at me and sat on the sofa, a sadness overcame her. "I'm a suspect, Lexi. Can you believe that?" She was near tears so I walked over and sat beside her.

"Why?" I asked and looked over at John. "What's going on, John? Why is Grams a suspect?"

John sat down in the chair. He looked deflated. "Your grandmother had a fight with the Swanson's Friday night."

Grams piped up, "It was that Mavis Clark. She just had to run her big mouth to the county cops and old man Jordan at the paper about a misunderstanding we had." She took in a long breath. "That's all it was. I drove them home. Would I have done that if I wanted to kill them?"

We all looked at each other. That bit of information could very well lead to suspicions. She had access to them when no one else was around. And a disagreement could be seen as motive.

"Velda, why didn't you tell me about this fight?" John asked.

The look Grams gave him could have shot holes right through him. "I didn't think it was important. We've fought a lot over the years, but that doesn't change the fact they were dear friends." She fought back tears. "There's no way I could kill them. I couldn't kill anyone. You know that John."

John raised an eyebrow. I hoped Grams didn't see it. She'd be even more heartbroken. I made a mental note to myself to ask him about it when I got a chance.

Grams finally got settled in after everyone left for the

night. The day had been hard on her, but luckily, the cops didn't take her in, just questioned her at the candle shop. I headed upstairs with the old case file under my arm. I knew it couldn't help, but I didn't know what else to do. I flipped through the pages. My eye caught a handwritten note scribbled across the bottom of one of the pages. It indicated that Grams had attacked Orvel Haynes after the disappearance of my aunt. Maybe that was what had John concerned earlier. Had she been mad enough to try to kill him all those years ago? Was it possible my sweet, loving grandmother had a dark side to her personality? I didn't want to think about that. I knew there had to be another explanation. Besides, I had other suspects to keep in mind too.

Chapter 11

On Friday morning I went back to the burial site in the woods. I didn't really expect to find anything, but the cops could have missed something. After reading the old case file of my aunt's disappearance, I didn't have much faith in these guys being any better.

I looked around the dig site and saw several footprints. That was expected since several people walked all over the place digging up the bodies. One print stuck out. The tread looked to have a big blank spot. Possibly a piece missing that left a hole where tread should be. I wandered on past the area to make a circle around the site. Whoever dumped the bodies could have come in at several angles and maybe left a trace.

I was about to give up when I noticed that strange foot print again. What was it doing this far away? I looked some more and noticed another one, headed up an overgrown trail. I decided to follow the trail to see if there were more prints. Fall leaves covered the ground, but some spots of dirt were still visible. If the killer walked over the patches of dirt, I might be able to find the tracks from time to time. I hadn't been in these woods since I was a kid and couldn't remember where all the trails led to. It was good exercise even if I didn't find anything. With all the donuts being consumed in this town, I had to keep up my physical activity if I wanted to keep my figure. Not that I had a rock star body or anything, but I do like what I have and want to keep it that way.

About an hour later, the trees started to thin and I could hear traffic. *Was I close to town?* According to

my fit tracker, I'd walked about five miles since
leaving the house. As the trees became more sparse, I
started to see buildings. I trudged on ahead until I was
at the edge of the woods. This trail had led to the back
of the mortuary. Movement out of the corner of my
eye grabbed my attention. I noticed the mortician
speaking to someone. The mortician was talking to
someone behind the tall wooden fence that separated
the front of the side road to the back of the mortuary.
He looked like he had been trying to close the gate
when someone stopped him. There was no mistaking
Orvel Haynes dishoveled hair do, so I knew it was him.
An arm reached out and grabbed him. He jerked away,
but I did notice a black sleeve on the arm of the
person behind the fence. I could barely see a silouette
though the cracks in the fence. I thought about
moving, but there was nowhere to get a better view
and I didn't want to make any noise and get caught
spying on them.

Baxter flew up behind me and scared the bejeebus
out of me. I ducked down behind a bush just as the
mortician turned towards my location. I peeked
through the bush and noticed the other person had
left. I assumed it was a man, but I couldn't be sure.
The mortician closed the gate, walked to the back of
the mortuary and disappeared through the door. *That
was close.* I looked up at Baxter, "You almost gave
away my position you silly bird!"

He replied with a squawk. I stood up and headed
back to the house. I was definitely going to be late for
work since it'd take over an hour to walk back. John
wouldn't mind since I had something interesting to
share with him, but the gossip box would be upset
with me for not being there to answer the phone.
Despite what was happening, I really was falling back
in love with the place. I loved these woods as a kid.
Peyton and I used to trample through them for hours

every day. The cool morning air felt good as I walked. It also gave me time to think. Why did that footprint lead to the mortuary, of all places? And who did it belong to? I had an appointment with the mortician for Saturday to pick up his report on the Swanson's deaths, so maybe I could snoop around and find out more about his mysterious meeting. I picked up my pace since I wasn't looking for tracks on the way back.

As I passed the place the couple had been buried, I glanced over and wondered if the mortician had something to do with it. He was creepy enough, but wouldn't he have better ways to dispose of bodies?

Chapter 12

The closer it was to Jake picking me up, the more nervous I became. I checked myself in the full-length mirror. I did look darned good if I had to say so myself. I decided on a black spaghetti strap dress that fit just snug enough to hug my curves. The material was wool-like but it was super soft. I wore my black low-heeled strappy sandals and a light denim jacket instead of the suit jacket. I hoped this made it semi-casual. Peyton had fixed my hair in an upswept look with curls hanging loosely around my face. *This should knock his socks off.* The doorbell rang at seven on the dot. I took in a deep breath, tried to calm my nerves and walked to the door.

Jake was hot! I had no idea a man could look so good in a black suit. He carried a bouquet of red roses. No date had ever given me flowers before. He placed them in my arms and extended his hand to escort me out to his car. To say I felt like Cinderella was an understatement. I started to suggest I take my car, so I'd have a quick get-away plan if I needed one, but seeing the passenger door already open on his red Miata changed my mind. Who was I to deny myself being treated like a lady, even if it was for only one night?

As he seated me in the car, he leaned over and kissed me on the cheek. I looked up to the most delicious smile I'd ever seen. My lips yearned for his at that moment. He had a sparkle in his eyes. "You look divine," he said as he closed the door and walked around to the driver side.

My head was spinning as we drove through town. I

couldn't imagine where we were headed until he turned down into the Seaside area. Cryptic Cove sits on a high ridge over the sea. The whole area is built into a cove, but areas are open to the sea. The tourist area had chic boutiques, fancy dining and condos overlooking the sea. Many tourists came strictly to this area and never ventured around the cliffs into town.

My heart started pounding at the thought of being taken to this area. Most of it was new, so it didn't exist when I was a kid and I hadn't had a chance to check it out since I'd returned. Jake reached over and touched my leg, "Relax Lexi. I think you'll enjoy this."

My nerves were excited and jangled at the same time. I still had my suspicions about the guy, but feeling his hand on my leg, I had to admit the warmth felt good. It was nice to be touched. I was having trouble remembering the last date I'd been on, much less the last time I enjoyed the pleasure of being touched by a man.

Driving down the narrow road towards the sea took my breath away. The lights from the piers and coastal mecca reminded me of a carnival. "Wow" was all I could say. I felt like a high school senior going to prom.

We enjoyed a beautiful candle-lit dinner at Antonio's. It was great for a romantic evening. Not so great for trying to get information out of him about the insurance policies. I don't know if he caught on to what I was trying to do, but he simply refused to talk about work or anything related to the case.

After dinner, we went to his condo. From the top floor, I could see out over the inlet. Sailboats and yacht's bobbled and gave the illusion of dancing lights across the water.

I was feeling pensive about being at his place. It wasn't a good idea, at all. He seated me on the sofa and poured me a glass of chilled champagne after he kicked on the gas fireplace and turned on soft music. "Did you bring me here to seduce me?" The question popped out before I could stop it.

"Only if you want me to" he said. The sly grin on his face told me he could do a good job at it. "You've been here a few weeks and I thought you might be missing a taste of city life."

"You'd be right about that, but how do you know anything about me?"

He laughed out loud, "I eat at the diner. I know you don't really belong in this town anymore and," he paused, "I probably know more about your history than you even remember."

"Oh yeah. The gossip box runs amuck in this place. I'm pretty sure everyone knows when everyone else goes to the bathroom."

He nodded his head in agreement.

I sat my glass down on the coffee table. "That brings us to you. The town's people don't seem to know much about you."

"Are you fishing for information again?"

"Maybe. You're very secretive."

"Well, I learned fast how this town is and decided I wanted to keep some things for myself. So, maybe I am secretive."

"Tell me about the Swanson's insurance policy."

He sank back into the sofa and ran his hand through his hair. I couldn't help but find it a sexy gesture. I could also tell he didn't want to discuss it.

"Do you work all the time?" He finally asked.

"Well, I did go to pre-law. I was being trained to be nosy, suspicious and live the job."

"That's no way to live. You need some down time too. Trust me, I know."

"Oh? Insurance sales must be hectic."

"We're not here to talk about work."

"I know, but this was a senseless crime." I watched his face. "You being an insurance guy and refusing to talk doesn't look good."

"I've told the cops what I can." He reached for the champagne to fill our glasses again. I sat there quietly. It was clear I wasn't going to get anything out of him.

"You're thinking again," Jake said as he slid closer to me.

"I know. I can't help it."

He smiled. "Maybe I can help with that."

Something was tickling my nose as I slept. I assumed it was Baxter, although he usually didn't tickle, he did more of a pecking thing. "Crap," I gasped as I remembered the night and not going home. I opened my eyes to find Jake laying beside me in his bed. He was propped on one elbow.

"Good morning." He said as he kissed my nose.

"We're naked!" I managed to sputter out.

"Yes. It happens when you take your clothes off." The smile lit up his face.

"I'm glad you find it so amusing."

"You were pretty amused last night."

"That was last night." I squirmed reaching for the sheet to cover myself with.

"Hmm, Are you trying to start something?"

"No!" I gasped. "I'm trying to cover up."

He kissed my forehead before getting up, grabbing my dress from the floor and tossing it to me. "I hate to run you off, but I have a meeting I'm going to be late for if I don't get you home." He said as he turned and went into the bathroom. I had to admit the view was pretty amazing.

The ride back to Grams' house was awkward. He was the perfect gentleman and escorted me to the door, but it felt like something was wrong. I'd never been run off at 5 o'clock in the morning, but considering my embarrassment over sleeping with him, I decided not to pry.

I headed upstairs, grabbed some clothes and hopped in the shower. I had too much to do today to keep reliving last night over and over in my head. My first stop would be the B&B. I probably needed a shrink at this point, but my best friend would have to suffice.

Chapter 13

Peyton squealed when she heard the news.

"This is not good news, Peyton. I'm not even sure I trust the guy."

"Stop being so hard on yourself. You deserved the date, and everything else. You've been way too uptight over everything."

"I know, but this could complicate things. I mean, what if he turns out to be the killer?"

"You don't believe that do you?"

"I don't know, but I know my track record with men and something is always hinky about the ones I pick."

"It'll be okay. Stop worrying about it."

"You're right, though. I did have a great time. Now it's time to get back to business. John needs help figuring out who killed that couple and I intend to help him."

"Did you learn anything last night?"

I tried to hide the grin on my face, but couldn't. "He knows which buttons to push."

Peyton threw a towel at me, "I mean about the case."

"No. He refused to talk about work or the case at all. I think he knew I was fishing for information."

"And he managed to dissuade you from your mission.

I'd say he has some mad *button pushing* skills."

"Oh hush!" I said as I grabbed a croissant.

"Are you two going after it, I mean going out again tonight?"

I could feel the puzzled look creeping up my face. "I don't know. He kinda rushed me out at five this morning and wasn't talking much. Of course, I wasn't sure what kind of conversation to have with a guy after a one night stand."

"You think that's all it was?"

"After the way he acted this morning, that'd be my guess."

I heard a buzzing sound and looked down towards the street from the balcony. A guy on a dirt bike zipped by. I looked over at Peyton, "I see that guy everywhere. Who is it?"

"Oh, that's Charlie. He's really sweet. People say he's slow, but I can't tell it. I think he was just homeschooled, so the town thinks he isn't educated."

"Well, he sure likes to ride around on that bike."

We both laughed.

"So, what's on your agenda for the day?" Peyton asked.

"I need to drop some files off at the office. Since it's Saturday, I don't officially plan to work, but I also need to go see the mortician and see what he's found out."

"He works on Saturday?" Peyton asked.

"He does this week. John said he was behind on some natural deaths from the county, so he hadn't finished up with the Swanson's autopsies."

"That man has always creeped me out. I swear he hasn't changed in twenty years."

"I don't remember him from childhood, but it's hard to mistake that hair of his from anyone else." I finished up by telling Peyton what I'd seen from the woods the day before. She agreed it sounded like something I should try to find out more about.

It was close to nine before I left the Bed and Breakfast and headed towards the center of town where the mortuary stood. It was a plain white building that looked more like a mansion. It occurred to me that most funeral homes had that same mansion look to them. It was sandwiched between an old three story hotel and the floral shop. *Convenient.*

Chapter 14

I walked in and looked around. No one was in sight, but this wasn't actually a busy office with people running all over the place. I noticed movement in a side door and turned to see Mr. Finche, the Assistant Medical Examiner coming out. His skin was pale and he had a pained look on his face. "Miss Danforth, how can I help you? Is your grandmother okay?"

"Yes, she's fine. I was," I stumbled on my words hating to ask the man for inside information, "I stopped by to find out what you've discovered about the Swanson's."

He scrunched up his face, "I can't tell you anything at this point. This isn't a good time to be here." He headed towards the door to escort me out. "I'm afraid I'll have to ask you to leave." I looked up to see the constable and county boys standing in the doorway. *Were they here for information or was something else going on?*

"John," Mr. Finche addressed the constable by his first name, "That was fast. Miss Danforth was just leaving."

A county boy spoke up, "I don't think that's a good idea?"

I looked at him confused, "Why's that, sir?"

"You seem to have a habit of showing up around dead bodies. We'll need you to stay here until we can question you."

"You questioned me already."

"This is a different matter. Please be seated and don't leave." He turned to Mr. Finche, "Where's it at?"

"This way," Mr. Finch replied. He glanced back at me as he escorted them all to the back.

John stopped and asked the county sheriff if I could go into the office instead of waiting here. He agreed and had deputy Will Hunter escort me to work. *What the heck was going on?*

About an hour later, John walked in with the county sheriff. Both had stern looks on their faces. John motioned for me to follow him into his office.

As I entered the door I asked, "What's going on, John?"

The sheriff was right behind me. "That's a good question, Miss Danforth." He said as he closed the door. "Have a seat."

I sat down in one of the chairs in front of the desk. John sat down beside me.

The sheriff walked around and sat behind John's desk and pulled out his notepad and pen. "Now, Miss Danforth, where were you this morning between five and eight thirty?"

I looked at John. He nodded his head, meaning I should answer the question. I skipped to the part where I'd taken a shower around six and headed to the B&B around seven. Peyton could vouch for me.

The sheriff took notes. "Okay, but where were you earlier than that?"

I shifted in my seat. I didn't want to tell him where I was but knew I had to, eventually. "What's this about? If you don't mind my asking."

The sheriff looked at John. "You haven't told her?"

John frowned. "I've been with you all morning. When did I get a chance to tell her."

"Okay," the sheriff said before looking at me again. "Orvel Haynes is dead."

"What?" I gasped out. "How? When?"

"This morning. That's why we need to know your whereabouts, Miss Danforth."

"You think I killed him? I'm working with John trying to find out who killed the Swanson's."

"I'm aware of that, but you were seen in the woods behind the mortuary yesterday. Maybe you were spying on him, waiting for your chance to kill him."

"That's insane!"

"Do you deny being behind the mortuary?"

I couldn't believe this was happening. And I couldn't imagine anyone saw me or who it was. "No, I'm not denying being behind the place, but I didn't kill him."

"Then why were you spying on him?"

"I went back to where the Swanson's were found and looked around, to see if we'd missed any clues."

"And?"

I looked at John, "Is this necessary?"

"I'm afraid so, dear. Just tell him what you were doing."

I turned back to the sheriff. "I saw a unique footprint. A piece of tread was missing. It was all over the crime scene. I kept walking around, even went past the spot where they were buried and noticed the same footprint, so I followed it and ended up behind the mortuary."

"So, you're an expert tracker?"

"No." I was starting to feel defeated and lowered my voice. "I think it was just luck."

"Luck? Miss Danforth, crimes aren't solved with luck. And what made you think my boys had missed something?"

I didn't have an answer. Not one I wanted to give him anyway. I couldn't tell him I thought maybe they were incompetent.

"I know crimes aren't solved by luck. But this case needed a break and I was trying to backtrack and cover all the bases."

He sat forward and stared at me. "This isn't looking good for you."

"How's that?" I asked, the heat rising in my voice.

"It's convenient that you're the one who found the bodies. Then when they get taken to the coroner's office, he mysteriously ends up in the incinerator before he can conduct the autopsy. What are you trying to hide?"

"Oh my god. Someone burned him?" I put my head in my hands. I couldn't believe this was happening.

"Now, where were you prior to your morning shower and going to see Miss Lewis?"

I looked at him. My head was spinning. "I was with Jake Donovan."

"At five in the morning? What were the two of you doing?"

I wanted to crawl under the desk or slither backwards out the door. This was one of my most embarrassing moments to date. "I, well, I spent the night with him. He can confirm that."

"Hmmm." That was all the sheriff managed to say.

"What? You think he'll lie about sleeping with me?"

"Anything's possible. Maybe you two were in it together."

"What the hell do you mean "in it" together? The only thing we were in is bed."

"Look, everyone knows he's been digging into old insurance policies. Maybe you two joined forces to cover your tracks."

"That's absurd!" I yelled it at him. I was through with being nice and cooperative. "Am I under arrest then?"

"No, but you know the drill—stay in town." He stood up and walked around the desk to the door. "We'll be in touch if we have more questions."

Silence and tension crept over the room after he left.

Tears were starting to form in my eyes. John stood up and patted my shoulder, "Don't you worry child, we'll get to the bottom of this."

"How could they think I did this? I don't even know these people."

I left John's office and sat at my desk. I pulled out my phone and called Jake. It went straight to voice mail. I tried three more times before deciding he'd turned his phone off. He probably didn't want to be disturbed during his meeting.

Chapter 15

At lunch, I told John I was going home. I couldn't focus on work and it was Saturday. Not many contacts we could reach on the weekend.

Instead of going home, I headed straight to Peyton's. I had to let her know what was going on.

Peyton poured me a glass of wine. "I know it's early, but I think you need this."

I sucked it down in one gulp. It wasn't very lady-like, but I didn't care. She poured me a second glass and I started telling her about the day. "I can't get through to Jake. His phone is turned off." My words trailed off.

"What?" Peyton asked.

"The sheriff said Jake was looking into a lot of old insurance claims."

"So? He's new. Probably just going through what old man Barnes had lined out and found some outdated."

"Yeah, but he rushed me out at five this morning and said he had a meeting."

"I know, you came by here this morning."

"What if he's the killer and he rushed me out so he could go, you know, do the deed?"

"You can't think that?"

"Well, the cops must suspect him or they wouldn't say that. I wasn't considered his accomplice until I told them I'd slept with him."

Peyton tapped her nails on the table. "You may be on to something. What are we going to do?"

"I'm going to go break into his office and snoop around."

"Really?" Peyton grabbed her jacket, "Let's go."

"I can't ask you to do this with me."

She handed me my jacket, "You didn't. I'm volunteering, so let's go."

"Don't you think we should wait til dark?"

"No, people would see flashlights on. Town is practically dead on Saturday afternoon. This is the perfect time."

We drove through town, and just as Peyton had said, it was practically dead. We drove around to the alley in the back. The insurance office's door was three doors from the end. I parked several stores down so it wasn't obvious if anyone saw us. As we approached Jake's door, it was open. "That's strange," I told Peyton.

She looked around and noticed the janitorial van. "Mr. Spidey." She said as she pointed to the van and the little old man gathering supplies.

"Who?"

"The janitor. That's Charlie's dad, Mr. Spidey. He's like the town janitor. He's nice enough, but a bit odd if you ask me."

"Is that his real name?"

Peyton giggled. "I don't know, everyone calls him that."

I thought for a moment. "Can you keep him occupied while I sneak into the office."

"Of course. I have the perfect distraction too. I'll discuss a mold issue with him." She winked before heading towards his van.

As soon as she had him distracted, I headed into the back of the office. This was my first breaking and entering, although technically I didn't break in. I just used a ready-made convenience, but I was still terrified of getting caught. My heart was pounding in my chest.

I inched my way up the hallway to the main office and reception area. I checked the plate glass windows to make sure no one was walking by before I slipped into Jake's office. Thank god it wasn't locked.

Inside was a different story, though. Most of his file cabinets were locked. I checked his desk drawers and found one full of files. Hopefully, there'd be something in them and I wouldn't have to break into a cabinet.

I flipped through several of the files before I heard the voices of Peyton and the old man. *Crap!* I said under my breath. *I need more time.* But more than that, I needed a way out of here without being seen by the janitor. I replaced the files and crept over to the door to peek out. They were headed into a restroom. Peyton looked around for me. I could tell she was nervous.

I made my move and headed out the door. I'd just

made it to the hallway when I heard the man's voice. "What the hell's going on here? Who the hell are you?"

I rushed down the hall as I heard him telling Peyton her mold problem was just a rouse.

She was right behind me when we reached the car. I was shaking and trying to catch my breath. Peyton was giggling, obviously, she found it amusing.

"What if he reports us to the cops, Peyton?"

"Ah, don't worry about it. Man hates cops. We used to climb his fence all the time and he never turned us in."

"But this is an office, not his fence."

It's a well-known fact that he has no use for cops and laws. Don't worry about it."

I started the car and we headed back to her place.

"Did you discover anything?"

"I didn't have much time, but I did notice that several people have left their money to Hayden's Ridge."

"The retirement village?"

"Yep."

"That's not all that strange, is it? I mean a lot of older residents live there. If they don't have kids, maybe they want it so other people have the luxury of staying there."

"Good point, but that Mr. Copeland is rude as hell. I can't see him letting that money go to improvements or to help other's out."

"You're right there. I wonder if he has control over the money?"

"I don't know, but I'll go see his assistant and see if he can answer any questions."

I dropped Peyton off and headed home to have an early dinner. I hoped Grams would be home so I could ask her if her friends ever discussed their insurance policies.

Chapter 16

It was starting to rain and the temperature had dropped, since the afternoon, leaving a chill in the air. Grams' house always had a soft glow and warmed my heart looking at it every time I pulled into the drive.

As I opened the front door I was hit with memories of childhood. This house always felt magical to me when I was a kid, but I had forgotten that as I'd grown older. After a month here it was finally flooding back in. I remembered how she used to have guests over for tea and appetizers. I closed my eyes and could faintly hear the chatter of their voices, soft music playing in the family room.

I went upstairs to my room and turned on the electric fireplaces Grams had installed to replace the old gas ones. The family room and each bedroom had one in true Victorian style.

This had been mom's old room and became mine after I was born. I put on some sweats and sat on my bed to look around. I wanted to remember more of my childhood and this home as it had been.

I looked around and spotted mom's old hat box in the corner. It was the only thing of hers that I'd brought with me when I came to Cryptic Cove a few weeks ago. I went over to pick it up and settled back onto the bed. I hadn't looked at it since I'd been back, since the day I discovered Grams was still alive.

She'd kept a lot of old photos, pieces of lace, and some crystals. As I dug under the photos I found a deck of cards and pulled them out. After inspection, I realized they were tarot cards. I couldn't believe my mom was into that kind of stuff. Surely she didn't practice black magic or something. She hadn't mentioned anything like this to me. I was starting to realize that I didn't even know her. It was bad enough I didn't know my Grams anymore, but I knew my mom. At least I thought I did.

I heard Grams enter downstairs. This was a good a time as any to ask her about these cards and the stuff my mom had been into. Maybe this was the reason we'd left Cryptic Cove.

I grabbed the cards and headed downstairs. Grams had turned on the fireplace in the family room, or great room as she'd always called it, the room where all the parties happened back in the day.

I went in and sat on the couch, sure she'd be in shortly. She came in with a tray of tea and cookies. She sat it down on the coffee table. I noticed two tea cups. *Was she expecting me to be waiting on her?*

Grams sat beside me and poured us each a cup of tea. I grabbed one of the cookies from the tray. My mind was taken back to childhood again. She would always let me and Peyton have tea parties and use her tea set instead of toy sets like other girls used. I had to smile as I nibbled on the cookie.

I looked at Grams, "How did you know I was joining you?"

She waved her hand in the air like she always did when strange things happened around her. "I'm a grandmother, dear. I know these things."

I pulled the cards out of the pocket of my sweat pants. "I found these," I said as I handed them to her.

"Oh, my. These were your moms. I wondered if she'd kept those."

"You knew about this?" I asked, a bit more shock in my voice than I intended.

"Of course. I'm the one who gave them to her."

"Aren't these for black magic or something like that?"

Grams crinkled her nose up at me. "Heavens no child. No one in this family ever practiced black magic."

"So, what are these for?"

Grams took a sip of tea. "It's a little like that self-help stuff. It's for finding answers so you can cope with the problem or learn new ways to deal with it." She paused, "A self-reflection of sorts. As a city girl, I thought you'd be open to other methods of helping people."

"What do you mean, other methods?"

"Well, do you think everything should be logical and realistic."

"No," I said before taking a sip of tea. "I've just never had experience with these...cards."

She patted me on the knee. "Maybe it's time you give it a try. Since these were your mother's, it's only right they belong you to now."

Baxter flew in and sat beside me. He was very interested in the cards. He was another strange occurrence around this place I couldn't quite figure out. I gave him a bit of cookie as I looked through the images on the cards. He pecked one of them. "Is this the card I need to read?" I asked him with a giggle.

He chirped.

"Okay."

Grams had left the room and returned with a book. She handed it to me, "You'll need this while you're learning."

"Learning?" I felt my eyes squint. I didn't intend to learn this stuff. I was just looking through them, but I might as well humor her and the bird too. I looked down at the card Baxter had pecked. It was The Fool. I rolled my eyes. *Yeah, that's me.*

I flipped open the book and found the entry for *the foolish card*, as I called it. It was quite fascinating. It indicated this card was about new beginnings, but what struck me the most is this. . .

The Fool encourages you to believe in yourself and follow your heart no matter how crazy or foolish your impulses may seem.

I crawled into bed that night with that reading still in my head. What did it mean exactly? Maybe it meant I could catch the killer if I followed my instincts. That was crazy since I didn't really have any killer hunting instincts.

I turned out the light and listened to the rain pelt the window.

Chapter 17

Monday morning I walked into the Constable's office. Three county guys were hovering around my desk, going through notes. "Hello" was all I could manage to say. They looked up at me, acknowledged I was in the room and went back to work.

The door to John's office opened and out stepped Jake. I felt the heat rising inside me. A mix of anger and remembering Friday night. He walked over to me with a concerned look in his eyes. "Where the hell have you been?" I asked through gritted teeth. "And why the hell did you set me up?"

His look turned to confusion, "What do you mean, set you up? I did no such thing."

"Oh yeah, what was that stunt you pulled getting me out of the way Saturday morning?"

He reached to touch my arm. I pulled back. "Lexi, I had a meeting. I told you that."

"Pfft. Likely story."

"This isn't the place to discuss this. Come by my office later." He said and headed out the door.

John walked over and suggested I go on to the candle shop. He wouldn't be needing me for awhile with all the other people using the office. He whispered, "The Swanson's were poisoned" as he escorted me to the door. I looked up at his face. He whispered again, "Go see Marcus Finche." Then he winked and opened the door for me.

I stood outside thinking how odd everyone was acting and wondering why the county guys were setting up shop in town now. I got the impression John wanted me to stay on the case. At least I hoped that's why he winked and mentioned Finche's name. I turned to head towards the candle shop and decided I'd stop off at the diner to see if Jake was in there. I wasn't waiting to go to his office just because he asked me too. I was too furious with the man to oblige him.

I sat down in the booth across from Jake. The waitress brought me a cup of coffee before I could rip into him again. I took a sip before looking at him. "Why did you set me up?"

Jake leaned in. "Why do you think I set you up? For what?"

"You know very well for what. You got rid of me so you could go," I lowered my voice so I didn't draw any more attention to me than I already had, "so you could go kill the mortician."

Jake sat back in the seat, confusion washed over his face. "Lexi, I didn't kill him. I was on a plane headed to my meeting."

"Yeah sure. How convenient."

"I was questioned this morning. That's why I was in the constable's office. I had no idea the man was dead until then."

"That's a likely story, but I know you were in a hurry Saturday morning. Maybe you just swung by the mortuary after dropping me off and shoved the guy into the incinerator."

"You're talking insane, Lexi." He crossed his arms over his chest. "You can check the time I left you and the time my plane took off. I think you'll discover I almost missed my flight. I didn't have time to do what you're thinking." He sat forward and reached to touch my hand. "The cops checked my timeline and they don't have any reason I did this. So why should you?"

Maybe he was right. I'd have to check his timeline, but I still wasn't trusting him. He'd been too secretive about everything since the day I met him. He was hiding something and I was determined to find out what it was.

I looked down at his arm laying across the table. He wore a black suit jacket. My mind started spinning. "Wasn't that you confronting the mortician Friday morning on the side alley?"

He pulled his arm back and let out a sigh. "I don't have to answer your questions." He stood up, threw a five on the table and left.

I sat there for awhile. Was it him I saw Friday morning while I was in the woods? Why wouldn't he tell me or deny it if it wasn't true?

I headed to the candle shop, hoping I'd get a few minutes of quiet before all the town gossipers started coming in. Looking inside from across the street I could tell it wasn't the place to be for having some quiet time. I headed to the mortuary instead. Maybe Marcus Finche would be forthcoming with some news.

Chapter 18

I'd seen Marcus Finche around town several times since I'd moved back home. For someone who deals with death, he always appeared to be a lively and charming man. He wasn't so lively and charming on Saturday when I'd came by to ask questions. I didn't expect him to be in much better spirits today.

The main foyer was full of flowers as it had been Saturday, although I didn't pay much attention to them then. A large counter stood in the center of the room. Mahogany, with intricate carvings. Several comfy looking chairs were splashed around the room. This room was very different than the back room he led me into. The back room had the warmth of an iceberg. Steel tables sat in the center, cold and barren. It had a macabre feel to it. I shuttered as I looked around at the sterilized equipment. Four steel doors lined the back wall. This was where death had its final say.

Mr. Finche tried to be pleasant considering the circumstances. "Come on into the office."

We entered a room in the back corner of the *death chamber*. He pulled out some papers, his eyes darted from them to me. He sat on the corner of the desk and looked at me with warm eyes. "I'm not supposed to share any information with you, not even at the request of John. The police are all up in arms," he said as he fluttered his hands around his head.

"I know, but can you at least tell me what kind of poison killed the Swanson's? Anything would be helpful."

He looked at the papers again before he stood and laid them on the desk. "I'm about to have tea, would you like some?"

I felt my eyes squint and my nose crinkle. What a time to offer someone tea. I looked at him, trying to read his expression. He had a glint in his eyes. "Uhm, sure, thanks."

He smiled as he left the room.

I looked to make sure he was out of sight before walking over to the desk and looking at the papers. I wasn't sure if he'd just given me permission to snoop around, but if the opportunity presented itself, why not.

There were two long chemical names on the paper. I pulled out my phone and quickly snapped a picture. There's no way I could remember them.

Just as I slipped my phone back into my pocket, he returned with two cups of tea and handed me one.

I took a sip and looked at him with a feeling like a cat who'd just gotten into the bird cage. "I'm guessing Mr. Haynes died in the..." my voice trailed off. I shuttered to think of being burned alive in a device meant to cremate people.

"Yes. I found him on Saturday morning."

"I thought those things didn't leave anything but bones and ashes."

"There's several settings on them. Whoever put him in there didn't know what they were doing."

"Oh. I see." I wasn't sure what else to ask since I had the names of the poisons. "I guess I've taken up enough of your time. Thanks for the tea." I said, setting the cup down on the desk.

"Let me escort you out." He said as he extended his hand almost touching my lower back. "I wish I could have been more help." He said as he cleared his throat.

"Oh, I understand. It's no problem. I enjoyed the cup of tea. Thank you."

"You're most welcome. If you think of anything else, just ask. I may not be able to answer, but it's nice to have lovely young women stop by." He smiled as he closed the door behind me.

I headed back to the candle shop. Maybe the customers had thinned out and I could do some research on the computer to find out what these words meant.

Chapter 19

I arrived at the shop just as Grams was being escorted out by the police.

"What's going on here?" I looked at Will Hunter, the cop who'd escorted me back to John's office on Saturday.

Grams spoke up, "Dear, would you watch the shop? They just want to ask me some more questions."

"For what?"

"It's a murder investigation, Miss Danforth." The taller cop said.

"You can't seriously believe my grandmother had anything to do with it?"

"I'll be fine dear." Grams assured me. "It's just a standard formality, as John calls it."

Anger rose up in my body. I went inside, grabbed the phone and tried to call John. How could this be happening? How could they suspect someone as sweet as my grandmother when sneaky people like Jake Donovan was roaming around and could very well be guilty?

A man answered the phone and I asked for John. I was told he wasn't in and could leave a message. "No message," I told the guy and hung up.

I flopped down into a chair. I thought this day couldn't get any worse. I heard the bell over the door jingle, looked up and realized it could. Half the town was standing in Grams' store. Shock covered their faces. I stood up and went behind the counter, placing my elbows on the top and rubbed my temples with my index fingers. Questions were flying at me and I didn't have any answers. I sure wasn't cut out to be any kind of cop.

After the crowd thinned out, I got on the computer to do some research on those notes I took a picture of at the medical examiner's office.

The first compound listed was Hippomane mancinella. I typed that in and discovered it's a tropical fruit, but it's poisonous. Odd. The second compound was a strong muscle relaxer used during surgery. That was also odd, but it was very clear the couple had been murdered. With those ingredients combined, it had to be premeditated too. No chance of an accident or coincidence. The couple hadn't gone to the Caribbean recently so it's unlikely they accidentally ingested this fruit. It could also be found in Florida, but I didn't know anyone who'd been there recently either. I'd have to ask John or Grams if anyone had taken a trip.

The door bell jingled just as I closed the browser on the computer. John stood in the doorway. He looked like he'd aged ten years in the past two days. His shirt was wrinkled and hung at his waist, untucked. His five o'clock shadow looked more like seven o'clock if there was such a thing. He walked on in, letting the door close behind him and sat on the edge of the chair. He placed his elbows on his knees and his head in the palm of his hands. My heart sank to see him in such a condition. I'd known John to be in a good mood, neatly dressed and looking on the bright side. There was no bright side to him now.

I sat in the chair beside him. "I guess you know they've taken Grams in for questioning?"

He slumped back in the chair. "Yeah, it's over the fight she had with the Swanson's the night of the bridge game. The cops are all in a tizzy about it."

"But it was just an argument. Why would they think she killed them over that?"

He had a strained look on his face like he didn't want to say what he was about to say. "She had a fight with Orvel Haynes twenty-five years ago."

"I was going to ask you about that. What happened?"

"I've never gotten all the details, but she conked him pretty good with a baseball bat."

"Oh, so they think she has a violent nature?"

"Yes."

"But, she drove the Swanson's home. Why would she do that if she wanted to kill them?"

John took in a deep breath, "Opportunity."

"You've got to be kidding me."

"That's what they think."

"Maybe so, but how could a woman her age kill them and then drag them off into the woods?"

"They think she had an accomplice."

"Are you serious?"

"Afraid so."

My mind was racing. I hadn't known my grandmother since I was a kid, but I knew she wasn't capable of harming someone else.

"So where do they think she got access to the chemicals found in their blood stream?"

John perked up some, "You found out about those? What are they?"

I grabbed the sheet I'd printed from the image on my phone and sat back down. "Well, one is a poisonous tree from the Caribbean, but it's also found in Florida. The tropical climate will allow it to grow. And the other is," I pointed to the name on the paper, "a strong muscle relaxer. It's used mostly in surgery situations."

John rubbed the stubble on his chin. "That's very interesting."

"Do you know anyone who's been to Florida recently and also has access to medications?"

"Not off the top of my head, but we definitely have a direction to go now."

I frowned at the memory of Jake being out of town over the weekend. Maybe he had a good alibi for the mortician's death, but did he have one for the Swanson's death? Did he have an accomplice who could've killed the mortician for what was discovered during their autopsy?

John picked up on my uneasiness. "Do you know someone who's been out of town?"

I fidgeted around, not wanting to give him a direct

answer, but he might as well know of my suspicions about Jake. "Well, Jake was out of town this weekend. What if he's been to Florida recently?"

"I think you should ask him," John said as he stood up.

"Me? I don't think that's a good idea."

"Why not?"

"Well, I kinda already accused him of killing the mortician and he has a good alibi for the time of death."

"I see."

"If I ask this, he might think I'm just trying to pin anything on him."

"True," John said as he headed to the door, "but that's how police work goes. I know you're not an official cop, but you have been dragged into being my secretary, of sorts. We can't play favorites."

I pooched my lips out. "I guess you're right. I guess that's why Grams is being questioned too."

"Yes, and with her and I being so close, the county guys wanted to deal with that themselves, but there's no reason we can't continue an investigation, between us." He said, pointing from himself to me. His mood had improved some since he came in. He pulled the door open, "I think I'll go get cleaned up. Let me know when you find out something."

"Will do."

After John left I sat and thought about everything. It seemed I was doing most of the legwork for him. I guess it was better for me to do it since he probably needed to stay close to the county police. And he wasn't much more experienced than I was in these matters.

Chapter 20

After Grams returned from being questioned, I decided to head up to Hayden's Ridge and speak to the assistant. The only new information I got from that visit concerned a set of triplets who own an herb shop close to Crystal Scents and grew herbs on their estate. I left there and headed to John's office. Mostly to be nosy. The county boys had cleared out. I found that odd and wondered if they'd caught the killer. John came out of his office when he heard me enter. "Where is everyone?" I asked.

"There's a big ruckus over in Jasper."

"Oh, what about?"

John sat down in the chair. "It seems there's some kind of terror alert, so all available law officers have been called out."

"What? Around here?"

"In the city. There's some big meeting about it."

"You weren't asked to attend?"

"I'm just a constable, but that does put this case back in our hands for now." He rubbed his chin. "I was thinking of having a town meeting tonight."

I sat in the chair, propped my elbows on the desk and my chin in my hands. "Do you think that will help?"

"Well, there's way too much gossip going around and the best way to get to the bottom of it, is to get everyone together and discuss it." John had a concerned look. "What do you think?"

He knew this town's people and that could be a blessing getting them together or an all-out war with all the gossip mongers in everyone else's business. "I think we should do it. I know these people can be a handful, but it may be the best way to get some things out in the open and maybe even draw the killer out."

"Let's do it."

I looked at my watch. "Do you think we have enough time?"

He stood up and laughed. "That's a silly question. It'll be all over town in less than five minutes."

I let out an unintended snort. He was right. It wouldn't take long at all to rally this town together.

I arrived at the community center at half past six. John was standing outside. He walked over to me. "I have something for you." He pulled out a flashlight. It was one of those large metal things. "You never wanted to be in a dark place without a light." He smiled, "And this one can also serve as a weapon. We don't know who's out there to harm us, you need something to keep in your car."

I thanked him, opened my car door and chunked it in the back seat.

The place was packed by seven. Half the town was in a shambles over the recent deaths, the other half were mingling like nothing major had happened. I know people deal with things in their own way, but this was a mixed group for sure. Mavis Clark planted herself on the front row. The smug grin on her face made me leery of her. She could be spiteful and a right handful.

John called the room to order and started explaining what little we knew.

He paused for a breath and Mavis took that as her opportunity to speak up.

"Constable Ballard." She started before being cut off by John.

"Mavis, call me John, this is not a formal meeting."

She rolled her eyes, "Very well. Is it true that several citizens in this town are suspects?" She turned and glanced over the crowd, stopping to look at Grams a little too long.

"Of course. It's that way in any investigation. We aren't here to discuss the suspects."

"Then why are we here? We all know several people who are capable of this. For instance, the Drakes grow the very poisonous plants found in the Swanson's bloodstream. And little miss hottie-tottie nurse has access to the drugs found in their system." She said as she started walking around the front of the room. "We all think her being a kind, loving soul is probably an act."

The people grew restless. Disturbed looks crossed their faces. Many of them looked around like they wanted to point fingers too.

Before I could stop myself, I stood up. "It's also a fact that Mr. Jake Donovan could be after the insurance money. He's also the nephew to Mr. Copeland who has access to those same drugs."

She turned and shot daggers through me with her eyes. "Oh, you young people, always want to blame the nice ones don't you? And how could you even think that after sleeping with him?"

I had no intentions of that little tidbit being blurted out to the whole town, even if they did know about it. "He's also taken several out of town trips over the past few weeks. He had easy access to Florida and the main plant used on them. And furthermore, neither he nor Mr. Copeland is here tonight."

She walked up to me. I feared she might smack me across the face. "That means nothing. You need to look at people who've had a long-standing motive to get rid of them."

"Like who?"

An evil grin spread across her face. "Well, for one thing, your Grams and the Drakes want to take over their store so they can split it amongst their shops."

"That's crazy!" I lashed out.

She turned to John. "Constable Ballard, is it true that Velda Wheeler has been called in for questioning?"

The ghastly look on John's face told me he didn't want to discuss this matter with her. He knew she had a way of turning things into an all out riot and since the people here fed on gossip and were already in an uproar, we'd never hear the end of it. He finally spoke, "Yes, several people have been questioned over the past few days."

She turned and glared at Grams, "Well, isn't it funny how people who have disagreements with her end up missing?"

Grams didn't flinch at the remark.

John spoke up, "Mavis, she's argued with a lot of people over the years. They haven't all disappeared or ended up dead."

"Are you sure they don't end up missing? She had a huge argument with the Swanson's right before they went missing and then were found dead. Half the town knew about it. Annnd," she drew the word out for emphasis, "it reminds me of a case twenty-five years ago. She had a huge fight in the town square with her own sister. Has anyone seen her sister since that day?"

Several people gasped in the crowd. Whispered chatter began between a bunch of them. I looked at Grams. That caused her to break. She was horrified and shaking terribly.

"Mavis Clark, you know good and well I didn't kill my sister. You're just here to start crap like you always do." Tears streamed down her face as she ran out of the building. The crowd grew louder and louder. John was trying to get it under control when I headed out the door to find Grams. I glanced back at Mavis who had quietly taken her seat. All I could see was the back of her head, but I was sure she had a Cheshire grin on her face.

I couldn't believe the woman could be that cold and cruel. Surely she knew how much Grams loved and missed Aunt Agatha. These women had known each other all their lives. I hadn't found out what was behind this rivalry, but I was going to. This outburst was completely uncalled for. The nerve of that woman just baffled me.

Chapter 21

Peyton called the next morning with the promise of coffee and pastries if I'd stop by to see her. I couldn't resist the offer of warm, buttery croissants. I'd take them over donuts any day. Plus, it would be good to run stuff by her that had been weighing on my mind since the town meeting.

We sat on the balcony and watched traffic go by after breakfast. The air was starting to get nippy with fall coming on, but the morning sun felt great on my face. I hadn't felt this peaceful in awhile. I figured it was the calm before the storm, as sailors called it. Whatever it was, I wanted to breathe it in and keep it with me always.

"You looked relaxed." She said.

I opened my eyes to find her staring at me.

"Enjoying the moment. When I get to work, the peace will be over."

"I know. And I hate to bring it all up, but I am dying to hear how the town meeting went."

I rolled my eyes. "Oh gosh, it was a complete fiasco."

Peyton's look was puzzled. "How so?"

I put my coffee mug down on the table and sat up straight in the chair. "Mavis Clark."

"Oh no, what did she do?"

"She pretty much accused everyone there, pointed out how each of them had means to kill the couple."

"Do you think she was right about any of them?"

"Well, several people do have means, but there's no motive to make them suspect."

"I see."

"How much do you know about the Drake triplets?"

She waved her arm, "They are super sweet. Neither of them would hurt a fly."

"Not even over their business?"

Peyton thought for a minute. "I don't think so. I mean, I know people can fool you, but I've known them all my life. They've always been generous and helpful to everyone." She paused to think again. "Their mom has been county clerk all my life too, and she's always been super sweet. My mom always hated dealing with the Magistrate's office, but I think she actually enjoyed going to the county clerks office to see Bessie."

"It doesn't hurt to keep them in mind," I said.

"Who else did Mavis accuse?"

"I was getting to that. It's pretty upsetting. She flat out accused Grams of killing her sister. Right there in front of everyone."

"Are you serious?" Peyton's eyes were wide with horror.

"Grams was so upset she ran out crying."

"They've had some rivalry going on all my life, but it's

never come to that. They actually act like siblings."

"How do you mean?"

"Oh you know, at each other's throats one day and best friends the next."

I thought back to what Grams had told me about Mavis having a thing for my grandfather before he and Grams married. That blew over, but then she had a thing for the mortician before he fell for my aunt. I guess old wounds don't always heal so easy.

Peyton filled our cups and sat the pot back on the tray. "Well, hopefully, John found out something."

"I don't see how. He was having a heck of a time controlling the crowd. Everyone was just insane." I took a sip of coffee. "But the real kicker is how Mavis kept defending Jake Donovan."

"Oh?" Peyton sat up in her chair. "How do you mean?"

"Well, when Mavis started attacking Grams, I couldn't help myself and had to speak up. So I started asking questions about Jake, explaining how sneaky he is, how he's out of town a lot and not to mention that he's Mr. Copeland's nephew."

"What did she say?"

I flailed my arm in the air. "Oh, he's a saint and a nice young man. There's no way he could possibly do it."

Peyton sat back in her chair. I could almost see the gears turning in her head.

"You have that look. What are you thinking?"

"That seems odd to me. She never takes to new

people in town. What if she and Jake are running some kind of scam together?"

"Why would they?"

"Well, money for one thing, but it's no secret that Mavis tries to buy up all the property in town. The Swanson's store is probably on her list and now she'll have a chance to get hold of it if only to keep your grandmother from getting it."

"That does make sense. I wonder what's so special about their store front? It's just a store in that row of store fronts."

"I don't know. Maybe we should check into it."

"I think so. Oh, I also need a favor from you later."

"Sure, anything."

"Jake is out of town again and I need to get into his office. Can you call the receptionist and find a way to get her away from her desk so I can sneak into his inner office?"

"Of course, I can. Just let me know when." The sly grin on her sweet face was priceless.

Chapter 22

I walked by Jake's office and saw the receptionist on the phone. I hoped Peyton was on the other end of the line trying to distract her. She stood up and walked down the hall. That was my opening to sneak inside. Luckily no one else was in the office.

I quickly made it across the main room and into Jake's office. I quietly shut the door behind me. My heart was racing. I'd never done anything like this before, except a week earlier, but the office was empty then. My legs were shaky as I walked to the desk. A few files were on top, nothing of importance, a few updates, and claims. I decided to look through the drawers. I didn't expect him to leave evidence in plain sight, but you never know.

The man was meticulously organized. He'd probably notice a paperclip out of place if I wasn't careful. I was about to give up when I found a file at the bottom of a drawer, hidden underneath magazines and other non-insurance content. I pulled it out. It was the Swanson file. I flipped it open. In the side notes were written Murder? My mind started racing. Did that mean Jake had intended to murder them? I quickly started skimming to find the beneficiary. My heart leaped out of my chest and I dropped the file when I heard, "Miss Danforth. I didn't know you had an appointment today."

Shit! There was no getting out of this one. I was caught.

I looked up to see Jake closing the door behind him. He turned to face me with a stern look on his face.

Surely he wouldn't hurt me in broad daylight, in his own office, but he could get to me at home in the middle of the night.

"Did you find anything interesting?" He asked as he approached the desk. He was towering over me again, like the last time I was in his office.

"No," was all I managed to stammer out. I bent to pick the file up. Before I could Jake was behind the desk and grabbed my arm.

"Leave it." He said. "I'll take care of it."

I jerked my arm away and made my way to the other side of his desk, to put distance, and an obstacle, between us. He had an amused look.

"A girl could get hurt sneaking into places she shouldn't be." His voice was coy with slight impudence. He was playing with me. I considered the thought he was one of those sociopaths, blends into society with ease but has a dark, evil side to them.

"I'm helping with an investigation. You know that."

He sat in the chair behind his desk, placed his elbows on the arm rest and brought his fingertips together in front of him. "Yes, but that doesn't give you the right to breaking and entering."

I couldn't help but notice how powerful he looked sitting there like that. "I didn't break in. The door was unlocked." I spat back at him. It seemed childish after I'd said it.

He stood and walked around the desk. I was shaking. He smiled at me as he took my arm and turned me towards the door. "I won't report this, but I better not catch you in here again going through my papers." He paused, I looked up at him. He reached out and touched my face. His hand was warm and felt good on my cheek. I felt my knees getting weak, remembering the night we'd shared together. He had warmth in his eyes. His lips parted, "In fact, it'd be best if you stop looking into this matter altogether before you get hurt."

He was teasing and threatening me at the same time. I didn't know how to react. He was such a pompous ass. Anger swelled up inside me. "Is that a threat?"

He removed his hand and flashed the coy smile again. "Concern," he said as he pulled my hand up and kissed the back of it. "Now, if you don't mind, I don't have time to play right now. I suggest you go help your grandmother make a candle or something else less dangerous than looking into murder cases."

He practically pushed me out the door and closed it behind me. The receptionist had a surprised look on her face as I walked past her. I hadn't intended for either of them to know I was there. I was such an idiot sometimes.

On the way back to John's office I decided to stop in the herb shop and see if I could find out anything from the Drake's. If they knew plants, they'd likely know where someone could get ahold of the one used on the Swanson's. They might even know how it could be used to poison someone.

Chapter 23

I was deciding my morning couldn't get any worse, but then realized when that thought pops up, something always gets worse. Jake had been...I wasn't sure what Jake had been. The more I'm around him, the higher on my suspect list he goes. He also keeps me off balance. I can't figure out this crazy attraction for the man. And this morning he was almost arrogant.

The stop by the Drakes shop wasn't any better. Peyton had told me how sweet they are. That may be true for Annie, but for some reason I rubbed Alice the wrong way and she had it in for me. She was rude as soon as I walked in the door. I know people don't always like the first time they meet, but I'd never done anything to her.

I returned to the office to regroup. I knew the phone would be ringing, but maybe that was the distraction I needed to stop all of these thoughts from invading my mind.

I also wanted to write out some notes about where the case was, who we still needed to question and what new developments had presented themselves. I'd also needed to head up to Hayden's Ridge again. I wanted to talk to the nurses on staff and hoped they'd supply some answers. Right now, it looked grim. *This case may never be solved*, I told myself.

I watched Jake enter the diner. My heart sank when he didn't look over towards my office. I don't know why I expected him to. I guess I hoped he was having second thoughts about the way he acted this morning. He sat in his usual booth next to the window. I secretly thought he did it to rub it in my face, even though that's the same place he always sat. I tried to get my mind back on work, but I found myself looking up every few minutes, hoping to find him looking at me.

About ten minutes later I saw Alice Drake entering the diner. She turned and glanced my way, or I thought she did. My heart skipped a beat when she walked up to Jake's table. I saw her laugh and then sit down. I had no reason to be jealous, but anger was boiling up inside me. I felt hot. I gathered my notes and decided to head to the retirement home. I couldn't bear to watch Jake having a good time with another woman, which was stupid. I didn't have any claim on him. Besides, he was a suspect, why did I care who he spent his time with unless they showed up dead. He could do what he wanted, I wasn't the least bit interested in him. So why did it bother me so much? Odd that I see her talking to Jake after I stop by to question her about poisonous plants. *Could they both be involved?*

After I returned to the office I found myself looking at the diner and watching Jake. How had I become so obsessed with the man? I needed a distraction so I pulled out my list of suspects. I didn't want to mark anyone completely off just yet, but after the visit up to the retirement village, it was becoming more clear the assistant, the nurses and the Drakes had no motive in killing this couple. I glanced across the street and kept Alice Drake's name on my list. She looked a little too cozy with Jake and I was still concerned about why she picked today to have lunch with him. Was it planned before I went to her shop to ask questions? There was no way to know.

I wanted to rule Grams' out too but had no hard facts to use for that. Mavis Clark was left on the list. The property in question was the only motive for her or Grams and it seemed unlikely that'd be a good enough motive for two older women. Besides, neither of them could physically lug a couple of bodies through the woods and bury them.

That left me with Bernie Copeland, the mortician, and Jake. An uneasy feeling crept over me at the thought of Jake. I didn't want it to be him, but he was definitely a high candidate on the list. I brought my hands up and rubbed my arms in a self-hug position. I couldn't shake the feeling. I sat back in the chair and had the daylights scared out of me from a man standing at the window staring at me. Once I caught my breath, I realized it was Jake. He looked vigilant in his stance with his arms crossed over his chest. I felt like some prey he was waiting to devour.

I motioned for him to come in. He walked through the door and took my breath away. I wish he'd stop doing that. There's nothing intoxicating about a man walking into a room, but when he does it, I lose myself, and my nerve.

"How long have you been standing there watching me?"

"Long enough to think about how beautiful you look after a night of making love."

I rolled my eyes. I didn't need to have this discussion,

didn't need him to reel me back in from being mad at him. "That's nice." I was short with him. "Is that all you wanted? I have work to do."

"You went up to Hayden's Ridge earlier."

"I did. What about it?" I started asking before it hit me, "Have you been following me?" I stood up and sent my chair rolling backwards.

"Maybe." He had that look again. "I thought I warned you about sticking your nose into this case."

"You did. I didn't listen." I wanted to stick my tongue out at him like a little girl would have.

"Then you need to start. You're in over your head Lexi. You're going to get hurt."

"Is that a threat? Another threat?"

"No, it's not a threat, just a fact."

"Well, the only person I see who is starting trouble with me over this is you. So, why don't you just admit you're behind it all."

"Look..."

I cut him off, "No, you look, I have a job to help do around here. My grandmother is a suspect in this mess and I'm determined to get to the bottom of it."

"I just don't want you finding yourself in the bottom of the ocean."

"So, that is a threat?"

Jake lowered his defensive stance, "Can we talk about this over dinner?"

I pulled my chair back up to my desk and flopped down in it, tapping my fingers on the desk. "What? And have you getting me drunk and taking advantage of me again?"

"I didn't take advantage of you!" His tone was gruff. I knew he hadn't, but I needed a way to throw him off balance so I could regain my composure.

"No, I don't want to have dinner with you."

"Lexi, you know I didn't make you have sex with me."

"What's it matter?"

"Because I want to hear you say it!"

"Can you leave now, before I have John come in here and throw you out of my office?"

"He's not here. It's just me and you." He said as he walked to my desk and placed his hands on the edge. He was bent, hovering over me. I'd gotten myself into this battle and saw no way of getting out of it. I looked up at him, expecting to see rage in his eyes. What I saw confused me. He was serious and concerned. Maybe he did care about me and wanted to keep me safe, but why play this game with me? Why couldn't he just come out and say it if he wasn't up to something? Were his eyes lying? Was he that good at deception? I had no way of knowing.

He straightened up and walked around the desk to stand beside me. He turned my chair around to face him, put his hand under my chin and pulled my gaze up to meet his. I felt my bottom lip quiver as I tried to speak. "Can you just leave, please?"

His charming, melt your heart, smile crossed his face, "Not until you agree to dinner."

Bastard, I thought. He knew he had me under his control. I knew he did. Why did I keep letting him do this to me? "Okay," I whispered. I felt like a frail puppy who'd been abused. He bent down and lightly kissed me on the mouth. I wanted to pull him in, to feel his tongue play around in my mouth. He pulled back, kissed my forehead and headed towards the door. "I'll pick you up at six." He turned to me as he pulled the door open, "It's casual." And he walked out the door.

I was left alone with thoughts of his touch and his sensuous lips. I flopped back in my chair. This is all I needed. How did I let him sucker me in again? I knew getting information out of him wasn't happening, so it was really a waste of time, other than the fact I liked his company... when I wasn't mad. And there's the fact that I find myself falling for him harder and harder each time I see him.

Chapter 24

I crossed the street and headed to the sandwich shop to meet Peyton for lunch. They had the best grilled ham and cheese, served with waffle fries. I was famished. As I stepped onto the sidewalk I glanced back over my shoulder at Jake's office, still in a tizzy about how everything had gone with him. I noticed Bernie Copeland entering the building. This piqued my curiosity. He could be going to check on insurance, but I had the eerie feeling it was about the Swanson's insurance claim, maybe even about their deaths. He looked back and saw me staring at him. He gave me a go to hell look and jerked the door open.

I started walking again, wishing he hadn't seen me. For everyone in this town to know what everyone else was doing at all times, there sure were a lot of secrets here. All towns have their secrets, and that makes a place fun and interesting, but sometimes secrets could be dark and foreboding. I had one of those feelings now as I wondered what Jake and Bernie were up to. I hadn't really considered they might team up, but if money was the motive, they very well could be in this together. They were both in the perfect job positions to run a scam on elderly people. I got sick to my stomach thinking of how Jake afforded his condo. Was it at the expense of people dying? I decided I probably wouldn't be having that sandwich now. My insides churned. I'd slept with the man. I was going on a date with him tonight. Talking to Peyton about my feelings were moot now. I needed to put these pieces together before anyone else died around here and Jake Donovan cashed in on it.

After having lunch with Peyton, we had pretty much ruled out everyone except Jake and Mr. Copeland. Jake was too secretive and Mr. Copeland was always on the defensive. At least he was with John and me. Peyton had talked to her friend who worked for the county, Will Hunter. He's the same guy who escorted me to the office on Saturday after the mortician was found dead.

He couldn't tell her anything, but she gathered that old man Copeland wasn't too happy with the county guys and their line of questions either.

She didn't like the idea of Jake being a killer or a con artist, but I told her we couldn't let our feelings stand in the way of getting to the bottom of things. I didn't like it either. I was having strong feelings for him and whether I wanted to or not I enjoyed his company. After not dating awhile, it was just my luck to be attracted to a con man and possibly a killer too.

I returned to my office, mostly deflated. Having such mixed thoughts about Jake was wearing me thin. He really was a charming guy. I guess that's what it takes to also be ruthless and to blend in with such an unsuspecting town.

I pulled my notes out again, looked them over and started over. I listed Jake and Bernie in one column, then listed the Swanson's and the mortician in another. It made sense about the couple being killed, their insurance money could be the motive. I couldn't figure out how the mortician fit in or how someone could cram him into an oven and burn him to death. Jake may be the bad guy here, but I couldn't see him doing something so heinous.

I fielded a couple of phone calls the remainder of the afternoon. It had been a long day full of dead ends and

I'd had my fair share of emotional turmoil. I decided to keep the date with Jake. Maybe I could trick him into telling me something or get more insight into his character. Besides, I was really hoping that a casual date meant beer and pizza. I could use both.

I locked up the office and left. I was about to pull out of the alley onto the main street and decided to go right instead of left to head straight home. I didn't need to spend the time to get fixed up for the date. With an hour before Jake would be by to pick me up, I had time to do a quick check of the mortician's house. Maybe there was something there to tie him into all of this mess.

The mortician lived up a secluded lane. It was creepy and reminded me it fit him perfectly. I pulled into his driveway. With the sun setting the place was darker than I was comfortable with. I fished my flashlight out of the back floor board. A gift I could truly appreciate right now.

I got out of my car and headed to the house. I saw a small basement light on in the right corner and held my breath. He probably left it on before he died. It was sad to see the lone light close to the ground, knowing the rest of the house was dark and gloomy, it's owner would never be returning. On second glance, I decided it was the evening sun glaring on the window. I let a breath out.

I eased my way around to the back of the house. I didn't intend to break in, but if I did, the back would be a better place than out front for any passersby to see.

I approached the back door, reached for the knob to turn it. Fear shot through me as it turned with ease. I should have been relieved at not having to break a window. My heart was pounding hard in my chest. I hesitated, trying to decide if I should go in. This was the craziest idea I've ever had. *Get a grip Lexi. Just go in, no one is here. The man is dead.*

I pushed the door open and stepped inside. The evening sun was casting shadows into the rooms down the hall from the kitchen. I headed down the hall, creeping my way, unsure of what I might run into. Thoughts raced through my head of ghosts haunting the mortician. Who better to haunt than a guy who deals with dead people. Sweat formed on my brow even though the house was chilly.

The hall led into a living room. Off to my right, I saw a door opened. It looked like a study or library. Luckily the evening sun was coming through the windows and illuminating the room well enough to see. I made my way across the room and peeked inside. There was a large desk in front of a curved window seat. The walls were lined with bookshelves. Various other pieces of furniture were set up in one corner of the room.

I padded across the floor to the desk. *People keep important papers in their desk.* I slid open the center drawer. It had an array of paperclips, pens, tape and other essentials. I opened the large drawer on the left-hand side. It contained some old newspaper clippings of my aunt's disappearance. I guess he truly was in love with her.

I moved to the drawers on the right. A noise startled me. I sucked in a breath, afraid to move. *Was someone in the house?*

The clock on the wall began ticking loudly, drowning out my staggering breaths. The seconds felt like an eternity. After a minute or so I quietly pulled open the drawer. It had old journals in it. I pulled one out and flipped through it. Nothing important. I glanced around the room. To my left were shelves and some drawers underneath. I stood up from the chair and went over to them. I squatted down and pulled one open. *Bingo!* This is where he stored his bills, receipts, and other important documents. I pulled out the file marked Insurance first. That was the best lead I had to go on to tie him into this case. I flipped through it as quickly as I could. The room was getting darker and I'd needed my flashlight. *Crap, it's on the desk.* As I stood up someone grabbed me from behind and slung me across the floor. I rolled and hit the leg of a table. Pain winced through my lower back. Before I could get up, the man was on top of me. The room had grown darker. I was in a frenzy trying to fight him off and couldn't get a good look at his face. I finally got a chance to kick at him and caught him in the gut. He bent over with the breath knocked out of him. I got to my feet and ran for the flashlight. He stood up, looked at me and laughed.

"That flashlight isn't going to do much."

I gasped. Bernie Copeland.

"If you come any closer, I'll hit you with it," I said as I pulled it back, ready to swing. "What the hell are you doing here?" I asked.

He laughed again. "Isn't that obvious? I'm trying to stop you from ruining my plans."

"What plans would that be?"

"Money, of course. I can earn a lot of money off these old people and I don't need you or that constable getting in the way."

"So, you did kill them?"

"I did."

"And the mortician. Did you kill him too?"

"Well, I didn't intend to, but he didn't dispose of the bodies properly. He had to be taken care of before he could rat me out."

"Maybe he wanted more money than you paid," I said, trying to buy some time so I could ease my way towards the door.

"He wasn't getting paid in cash. I was just keeping his secret for him."

"What secret?"

"What's it worth to you to know?"

"Nothing. I don't care what his secret was." I'd inched my way to the edge of the desk, it was almost a straight shot to door if I could just run fast enough.

"Oh, you should, my dear. A lot of people in this town would be interested in his secret." He waved his hand in the air, "The secret this house holds."

He'd piqued my curiosity, but I didn't have time to play games. I knew he'd kill me if I didn't get out of there. I bolted towards the door. He lunged forward and tackled me into the bookshelves against the wall. My breath escaped me and pain radiated through my body. My arm came down with the flashlight and caught him on the side of the head. He staggered backwards. My vision growing darker. I was sliding down the bookshelf. He came at me again. I swung the light again, hitting him in the same spot. He fell backwards crashing into the solid round table behind him. I slid down the bookcase, my back felt like razor blades were gashing me open.

 I closed my eyes tightly, trying to will the pain to go away so I could get up. I blinked my eyes open and saw Jake standing over me. Was he here to finish what Bernie had started? I didn't have the strength to fight him off. My last thought before everything went black was I would die in this house.

Chapter 25

I heard voices in the distance and finally forced my eyes to open. I was surrounded by red roses. At least heaven is beautiful I thought, but I didn't think it was supposed to come with a pounding headache. I tried to raise up and look around. I felt something on my arm and looked to find an IV attached to me. I wasn't dead. How did I get here?

As my vision began to clear, I looked around and saw dozens of vases of roses around my hospital room. A tear glided down my face at the thought of people caring for me that much. I turned my head to the left. Jake stood up, walked over and took my hand. "Hey you. I was wondering when you would wake up." His infectious smile beamed across his face. His eyes misty with tears.

"What happened? I thought you killed me."

He leaned forward and kissed my forehead. "Why would I kill you?"

"Because you were in on this with Bernie."

He pulled the chair up so he could sit by the bed. "I have some things to tell you about that."

I looked at him, trying to read his face. "What is it?"

He let out a sigh and squeezed my hand. "I'm an insurance investigator, Lexi."

"What? You led me to believe you were some sneaky bastard in with this scam with your uncle. Why did you do that? Why didn't you just tell me?"

"I've been undercover here for four months. I couldn't risk having my cover blown."

"Where is Bernie? Did you get him?"

"He's dead."

I gasped, "Oh no, did I kill him?"

"No, he fell and hit the back of his head."

"How did you find me?" I could buy the story of him being an investigator, but how did he know to look there for me?

He let out a soft chuckle. "Yeah, that. I hired someone to follow you."

"What? Who?"

"That guy, Charlie."

"The guy who's all over the place on his bike?"

"Yep. I knew since he liked to ride around all day anyway, you'd never pick up that he was following you."

I shook my head and laid back on the bed, my mind was reeling with everything he'd just told me. He noticed the concerned look on my face.

"What's wrong?"

"Was going out with me part of your undercover investigation?"

He smiled, "No, that was me going out with a woman who rocks my world."

My heart melted and relief washed over me knowing

he wasn't the bad guy. I felt guilty for having so many suspicions about him, but at the same time, he had misled me into thinking he was in on it. I wasn't sure how I felt about that.

I awoke the next morning with sunlight beaming through the window. My head wasn't pounding as bad as it had the night before. That was a good sign. Maybe the doc would spring me from this joint today. I rolled over and stared out the window. So much had happened over the past month that I hadn't had time to breathe. After taking the job with John, I hadn't even had time to settle into my new life. I thought about Jake and secretly hoped he'd be a part of it. He had been on assignment in this town so he'd probably be heading back to his own world as soon as the state and federal investigation was over. My heart pinched at the thought.

I heard the door open and turned to see which nurse was coming in to poke around on me this time. My heart fluttered seeing Jake roll a cart through the door. I sat up in the bed, "What's this?"

He walked over and kissed my cheek. "You still owe me a date."

I crinkled my nose. "So, hospital food counts as a date?"

He smiled. *Yeah, I could get lost forever in that smile.* "Well, it could, but you're in luck, I happen to make a pretty good breakfast."

"You cook?"

"I can hold my own in the kitchen. You would have found out on our last date, but I had to leave town early. Remember?"

"I do," I said as he helped me out of the bed and escorted me to the chairs he'd sat up by the window with the cart between them as a table. I looked down at the hospital gown I wore. "I hope this is what you meant by casual. It's not exactly my best outfit."

He stopped and looked at me. "You're beautiful." He had a gleam in his eye.

I couldn't be sure but I think he really thought I was beautiful with my hair messed up and wearing ugly hospital garb. "You need an eye exam."

He pulled the cloth cover from the cart and pulled out a vase and single yellow rose for the centerpiece. There were two covered plates, a bowl of fruit, coffee, and orange juice.

He pulled the cover off and revealed miniature pancakes, sausage links, and scrambled eggs. My stomach began to rumble. I was starving. I was skeptical about his cooking expertise, but it did look and smell good. I figured it was at least as good as hospital food. I prepared my pancakes and took the first bite. I was wrong in my assumption. The man had a knack for pancakes. I don't know what he did to boring eggs but they were divine. "Oh my gosh. These are delicious. What did you do to them?"

"It's a family secret." He said as he winked.

"Some girl is going to be lucky when she catches you."

Jake put his fork down and looked at me. "Is there a chance that girl could be you?" He had a sincere look in his eyes.

I felt uneasy, not sure how to reply. "Aren't you

leaving here as soon as this case is wrapped up?" I turned my face towards the window, afraid the truth would hurt more than I wanted to admit.

"Not necessarily. The town still needs an insurance agent, and I seem to be qualified for the position."

I turned to face him. I'd heard people talking about their hearts doing this pitter-patter thing, but I never much believed it, until now. I wasn't sure what I was feeling or why I was even feeling it. The thought of him staying in Cryptic Cove made me happy, happier than I expected.

"Are you okay with that?" He asked, breaking the silence.

"I like that idea." I couldn't see myself, but I was sure my face had blushed.

The doctor came in after we finished eating. He said I only had a mild concussion and could go home. He also said I should take it easy for a few days. That would be great after the craziness of the past two weeks. The release papers were done by eleven and I was free to go.

As Jake pulled his car out of the parking lot to take me home, I started going over things in my head again. I looked over at Jake, "What was the big secret between Copeland and Haynes?"

Jake looked puzzled, "What are you talking about?"

"Bernie said he killed the mortician for not disposing of the bodies. He also said Orvel Haynes had some big secret the whole town would be interested in."

Jake shrugged his shoulders, "I don't have a clue."

I tapped my fingers on the car door as we drove through town. I perked up, "Go to the mortician's house."

"Why?"

"There's something there. I know it."

"Lexi, you just got out of the hospital."

I waved my hand and blew him off, "I had worse injuries jumping rope as a kid. We need to go find that secret."

"You need rest."

"Fine, I'll go myself."

He looked over at me and shook his head. "What am I going to do with you?"

I grinned at him, "You're going to take me to the mortician's house."

Chapter 26

John was working on the investigation when we arrived at the mortician's home. Most of the evidence had been bagged and taken away. He was just looking around a bit more to make sure they'd left nothing behind.

I looked over to the window I'd seen the night before. It still seemed to glow and no sun was shining on it. I grabbed Jake's arm and told him I wanted to see the basement.

We went into the kitchen and found the door to the basement. It was full of boxes and furniture. Only a narrow path led through it. We wandered through the maze until we came to where the corner window should be. I looked at Jake, "There's a corner window on the outside of the house. It should be right here." I said pointing up to the corner.

A sheet of plywood stood in the corner. Jake pulled it out and discovered a door behind it. John came up behind us and startled me. I let out a gasp. "Sorry, I didn't mean to sneak in, just wondered what you two were doing down here."

I pointed, "We've found a hidden room."

John stepped up to help Jake get the metal door open. The hinges opened easily. John looked inside, "Oh my god!"

I peeked around him to see what he was looking at. A woman stood in the middle of the room, "Where's Orvel?" she asked.

John looked at me, shock spread across his face. He turned and stepped into the room. "Agatha? Is that you?"

My heart skipped a beat. *Could my aunt be alive after all of these years?* What was she doing locked away in the basement? My heart cringed at the thought of that creepy bastard keeping her all this time.

"Agatha, it's me, John Ballard." He stepped closer.

Her mouth fell open as she reached out to him, "My god John. I can't believe it." They embraced each other in a hug. She stepped back, "Where's Orvel?"

John looked at her. We could all see the concern on her face, she was lost. He finally spoke, "Orvel's dead. He was killed a few days ago."

Agatha sat on the bed and placed her face in her hands. She was clearly upset over the news. She looked up finally, "I knew something was wrong when he didn't return on Saturday."

We stepped further into the room. It was well decorated and cozy. If a prison can be cozy.

John walked over to her, turned and pointed at me. "This is your grand niece, Lexi."

Agatha looked up, "Katherine's daughter?"

"Yes," I said.

"Velda? Where is Velda?"

John reached out for her, "Come, she'll be so happy to see you."

Agatha took John's hand so he could lead her out the

door. She stopped in the doorway and turned to look back. Tears ran down her face. "I've been here so long." She looked back to John. "I don't know what the outside world is like anymore."

John put his hands on her shoulders. "A lot has changed, but you have family who loves you and you'll get through it.

Agatha stood outside looking towards the sky with the morning sun on her face. She looked like an angel. An angel who'd been gone from the world far too long. She was finally going home, finally free. Baxter flew in and perched in a nearby tree. I saw her turn towards him and smile.

We returned to the hospital with Aunt Agatha. John insisted she get checked out. The doctor took her in immediately and wanted to run a bunch of tests since she hadn't seen a real doctor in twenty-five years. The reunion between her and Grams was emotional. They hugged and cried and then cried and hugged some more.

Grams insisted I go get some rest because of the concussion. She'd been cooking all morning for my homecoming, but we decided to save the food for my aunt's homecoming instead.

Jake told Grams he'd watch after me. I expected that to mean he would stay at the house with me. Instead, he took me to his condo. He said I could stay as long as I needed to so Grams and Aunt Agatha could spend time together once my aunt was released from the hospital. I knew they would need time alone, but it would be strange staying with Jake. I didn't know what he would expect. Were we a couple? I didn't know. He'd been great, but I wasn't ready to jump into anything serious just yet. Luckily, he had a small guest bedroom I could stay in. Although, every time I looked at the couch I remembered what happened there the week earlier.

I stood staring out across the ocean. He had a great view. I heard movement behind me and turned to see Jake sitting on the couch, watching me. He patted the seat next to him, "You're supposed to be resting. Come sit down."

I walked over and looked at it. "This couch was trouble the last time I sat on it."

He reached for my hand and gently pulled me down to sit beside him. He tucked a loose strand of hair behind my ear and then kissed me on the nose. "You have a concussion. I promise to be a perfect gentleman. I can't promise not to kiss you though," he said as he took my mouth with his.

He sat back and cuddled me into his arms. It was the right place to be.

Ω

If you've enjoyed this short mystery, please go back and leave a review at Amazon or wherever you obtained your copy. I love hearing from my readers. Thank you and God bless!

Don't forget to visit my website and sign up for my mailing list to stay up to date with new releases: http://kpstafford.com

About the Author

KP has always loved creative writing, but it wasn't until late 2014 that she stepped away from her freelance writing career and started pursuing fiction writing full time.

She's a mom,Nana and musician's wife. Music is a huge part of her life. When she isn't writing, she's out living the music life with her husband.

She's always loved things mysterious and a bit kookie. Vincent Price made a big impact on her when she was a child, as did The Munsters and The Addams Family.

She now tries to bring her, sometimes twisted, blend of mystery and reality to life in her books.

If you've enjoyed her work, please visit her website and get on the reader's list so you can receive advance notifications, discounts and reader's only specials.

http://kpstafford.com